for Dave and LoJean
with love

Verlin

March '85

After Goliath

BOOKS BY R. V. CASSILL

Novels

The Eagle on the Coin

Clem Anderson

Pretty Leslie

The President

La Vie Passionnée
of Rodney Buckthorne:
A Tale of the Great American's
Last Rally and Curious Death

Doctor Cobb's Game

The Goss Women

Hoyt's Child

Labors of Love

Flame

After Goliath

Short Stories

The Father and
Other Stories

The Happy Marriage
and Other Stories

After Goliath

R. V. CASSILL

Ticknor & Fields • New York
1985

Library of Congress Cataloging in Publication Data

Cassill, R. V. (Ronald Verlin), date
After Goliath.

1. David, King of Israel — Fiction. I. Title.
PS3553.A796A68   1985   813'.54   84-16225
ISBN 0-89919-325-0

Printed in the United States of America

S   10   9   8   7   6   5   4   3   2   1

THIS BOOK IS FOR
GEORGE P. ELLIOTT
AND
MARY EMMA ELLIOTT,
THE VALIANT PAIR.

And the happiness of the spirit is to be anointed and through tears to be consecrated as a sacrificial animal. Did you know that?

— Nietzsche, *Thus Spake Zarathustra*

Death is the last, and in that respect the worst enemie.

— John Donne, *Sermons,* no. 1, vol. 5

The Characters at a Glance

◆

Abishag	Famed as "the virgin" brought in by physicians to keep King David warm on his deathbed.
Abishai	Joab's milder brother.
Abner	In the war between the House of David and the House of Saul, Abner achieved some celebrity for his shuttle diplomacy. Womanizing complicated his efforts as an evenhanded peacemaker, but he might have gone further as a diplomat were it not for Joab's speed with a blade.
Absalom	King David's handsomest, most charismatic, and most ambitious son. A go-getter born for trouble.
Achitophel	Plotted with Absalom to oust King David from the throne. According to John Dryden, a great wit, and "Great wits are sure to madness near allied / And thin partitions do their bounds divide."
Adonijah	Son of King David and wife Haggith. Impatient to become king at the point of his father's death.

Amasa	Cousin of Joab and Abishai. Might have gone further with his military career were it not for Joab's speed with a blade.
Amnon	King David's son. His sexual preference was rape.
Bathsheba	Originally the wife of Uriah the Hittite. Subsequently King David's wife and mother of Solomon. Picture a famous — now fattening and aging — American film star. Picture her bathing!
David	Warrior and sweet singer. Second king of Israel. Born in Bethlehem, son of Jesse, from whose lineage sprang Jesus of Nazareth. Most popularly known for killing the unlucky Goliath and for composing magnificent psalms.
Goliath	The big fellow. Thought by some modern endocrinologists to be a victim of multiple endocrine neoplasis. Since this is not a medical novel, he has only a peripheral role.
Hushai	A loyal friend to King David. In the parlance of the modern espionage community, a mole.
Itai	One of King David's generals. The bravest of the brave; the dumbest of the dumb.
Jehoshaphat	Called in Scripture a "recorder." Probably the epithet was intended to disparage his gifts as a creative writer.
Joab	King David's indispensable hit man. Military leader and theorist. His greatest success might have been as a free agent in the perpetual wars of the time. A fast hand with a blade.
Nathan	Eupeptic killjoy prophet with a moral sense far in advance of his times. Picture an idealistic, activist chaplain at a small Ivy League university.
Samuel	Dyspeptic kingmaking prophet, who brought both Saul and David to their thrones when the Israelites demanded they have kings like other folks.

Saul   First king of Israel after the time of the Judges. Given
              to black moods and depression in his later years. Dis-
              owned by God and the prophet Samuel for being soft
              on the enemies of Israel.

Shimei   Foul-mouthed paladin of the House of Saul.

Solomon   King David's son and successor to the throne. Nathan's
              pride and Bathsheba's joy.

Tamar   The object of her brother Amnon's predilection for
              rape.

Tamar II   Absalom's daughter, named for his despoiled sister.

Uriah   A gung-ho junior officer in the army commanded by
              Joab.

Prologue

———◆———

Joab

———◆———

AN OLD soldier. Home from the wars. Sitting under my own fig tree, near the grindstone in my own back yard. Finally I can speak frankly. Of one and all.

King Saul, you should have seen him, I tell my recorder, Jehoshaphat. Saul was a very tall gentleman with extra long arms. Long arms are good for a fighter. But he had a perplexed look toward the end. King Saul was very noble. Measure him as a man, and you might well conclude he was nobler than King David. Yet for me there is but one King. A great king is not just a man, however noble he may be in personal nature.

Jehoshaphat would like to get down all my thoughts on what it takes to be a great king. He is trying to expand from his specialty of military history. He hopes to get some of his present work included in the Bible.

Luck, I say. I would name King's main feature to be his luck over a long period. That is what makes for good policy and a successful reign. King had his reasons for every move he made.

Which a king ought to. They were just not clear to him most of the time until pointed out, and by the time they were pointed out, as often as not he had drifted on to another tack where he needed purely contradictory reasons. But with some steadying, he has lucked out consistently to this present day. He has even been lucky in love, though that Bathsheba has been more than he originally bargained for.

Jehoshaphat chirps, "Would you say that in times of uncertainty the Lord sent King David a guardian angel to clarify a course for him?"

Now that is a chuckle. Look at me. Do I look like any angel to you?

Now that I am relieved of duty, Jehoshaphat has found me easygoing. But not many men can look at me square. I am so ugly they are afraid I will catch on to how ugly they think I am and resent it. I am just about the only man in this city who keeps his hair cropped short, which I cut with my own knife. Beard likewise. Short, bristly, and growing spotty from a disease I got by wading in unclean blood. There is something about my eyes I don't like very much myself. But peace-loving for all that. Here in my back yard.

Jehoshaphat sort of squints at me obliquely, and what he writes down is that King "could count on Joab's vigorous support in emergencies." He's got style.

A lucky king is one who can keep the whole ball of wax in one lump for the longest time, I opine. Kingdoms as well as life itself are full of items that in no way fit or stick together by themselves. Items that are ridiculous as well as heroic, plain as well as complicated, stinky as well as majestic, and so on, until you have not left out a single per cent of what life is bound to be.

I will tell you, King did things ever so often that would disgrace a common man. Silly things that would make a red-ass baboon chuckle. And had things flung in his teeth you or I would not be able to swallow. A king had better have a stomach like an ostrich. But such items are only a certain per cent of being a king others will not live up to for a long time. You may find I like to dwell on the chuckles I have had on him. That is the way of old soldiers.

But since it's free, I intend to be also fair. Though he gave us no laws worth spitting on, consider the first-rate psalms he made up. Psalms are the superior of laws, being out of reach of lawyers and their quibble for all time to come. King's lamentations will stick in people's minds long after they have forgot how he always fudged some political profit from his sorrows. Politically, he was some stud. That goes without saying.

A great king is he will stick in mind, even his contradictions. He has entertainment value, which is the greater part of either history or religion.

The psalms are truly praiseworthy, Jehoshaphat says. He goes on writing, whether he is taking my point or not. Which probably not, for with his brows knotted up piously, he says, "They make us forget his merely human foibles."

I am saying don't forget nothing. Life is one hundred per cent, and there is no use trying to live it fifty, seventy-five, or even ninety-nine per cent, because the rest will always catch up, though you intend to ignore it.

"You are saying [Jehoshaphat tells *me,* neglecting I am the one who is supposed to have said it] that our King David did not fail to meet life steadily and see it whole."

A nice way of putting it. Which is what scroll mice are for, and every man should be good at his trade.

But anyone who wants to hear the inside on the fight with Goliath, the naughty stuff with Bathsheba, Absalom's rebellion, how we handled the traitors Abner and Amasa, and other famous matters I have knowledge of, should get it from the horse's mouth. The trouble is that if such stuff should leak into the Bible, somewhere along the line someone will have taken the spice out of it. In my understanding, the Bible is supposed to deal with what is right and wrong. I did not hire on to settle matters of right and wrong but to do what was needful. At any given moment, whatever were the odds.

The Bible editors will reduce all the blood and grief to a body count of Philistines or Syrians and mumble their way through the sex parts. There was much sex happening in my time. More than is to my taste, as a matter of fact, though I am one to enjoy a smutty story if there is a chuckle in it. Man is not more often comical than when bent on pleasuring himself with women.

I agree the Bible should not deal with pud-pulling, sheep-fucking, and faggotry, though they are a per cent of life also, and some crazies continue to prefer them, as we keep hearing. To keep my account accurate, I will deal with such matters as they affect major events and participants only.

◈

In the long run, I have been more faithful to King than you might think he deserved. Though I chuckle, I will never deride him. But I will tell you straight out that in his early days he didn't know beans about handling his job. It is a fact he asked old Samuel if he was supposed to "carry on" with what he had learned from being around King Saul.

Samuel was like me. No prettier. And also a hard-liner on what was required to be done. He laughed King to scorn. Saul had struck out. The Lord had put him down for cause. A very unlucky sort of king.

"You *make it up,* boy," is precisely what the old fellow told him. "Day by day you invent how to be king."

"I still don't see how." King had little to go on beyond taking care of sheep.

"By *doing* it," Samuel roared. He didn't know, either, but being a big-shot prophet, he had to make out he was giving a reliable answer. "You imagine a king by being a king. You be it by imagining it. You're all alone out there. When in doubt, do something. If you do it as a king, the reasons for it will come later."

Though he had to swallow what Samuel laid on him, King still saw the catch in what he was being told. It gave him a lot of freedom with his mistakes, and he was willing to accept what came to him for them. But he foresaw truly he would damage those he drew along with him. His people.

That was the least of Samuel's worries. Screw the people, was his view. Judges weren't good enough for them! Other nations had a king; what was lacking in Israel they could not have one as well? "They want a king," he said. "I'll give them a king! See how they like it."

Which is pretty much all he offered for King to start from, and much trouble from all of Saul's people still hanging around wanting to get their bite on the Big Tit again by treasonous means. Saul's man Abner almost tipped over King's cart, and would have if I hadn't been there to prevent it.

I guess part of what King made up was me. To do the needful dirty work for him. Which is the part of my trade I will get no glory for, in the Bible or elsewhere.

Fine. The fact is I want King to have all the glory he deserves for doing as well as he has against the hundred per cent that real life tosses at kings and lesser.

But I will not say he didn't fail. However the scroll mice may write it up, those are not my words.

With some help to steady him, he was a great king, for sure. I never said he was adequate.

The Hittite's Wife

———◆———

Many there be that say of my soul, There is no
help for him in God. Selah.
— *Book of Psalms 3:2*

As We Look Back from Right Here and Right Now at David and Bathsheba

———◆———

SEE HER WITH the king's eyes. Make the crucial distinction between an ordinary hard-on and a royal erection.

It is late afternoon in the sultry little garden not a hundred paces from the palace wall. Bathsheba is bathing. Much of her garden is already in shadow. Her languid peacocks are belly down in the shade of the flowering bushes, their long necks writhing with the stir of peacock dreams. The maid who has brought linens and towels from the house is a shadow herself. Her skin is tawny and her clothing is dark.

But the tub in which Bathsheba crouches is in a patch of full sunlight. Amid the dark greens, blue shadows, and umbers it is a pool of liquid gold. The maid who now dips and pours tepid water down the shoulders and luxuriant back of her mistress seems in awe. Such service partakes of a profound female mystery, and the woman Bathsheba knows herself to be its center — to be, in fact, the center of a concupiscent universe.

Dripping precious rivulets, she rises. Muscle and bone move

as if they were lifting treasure out of the scented water. She flirts with the sun, arching her womanly front to tease it down. She poses, as if the sky itself were a lens through which she is being watched by celestial observers.

In fact, she is being watched by the king of Israel, who *happens* to be pacing the roof of his palace, *happens* to glance down into the neighboring garden where, before this, he has sometimes had occasion to admire the strutting of her spoiled peacocks.

Should he not pause at the sight of Uriah's wife in her wet splendor? Not feel the pump of desire lift his kingly member?

❖

Any pimpled boy, or soldier, farmer, shopkeeper, tax man no doubt would have got it up if he had seen Bathsheba in that ideal setting. Lust is the proper response of the male creature to his needs. But a king, by definition, cannot have *pure feelings* about women or anything else.

Watching the dusky maid fluff her towel up the narrowing valley between Bathsheba's thighs, King David could not simply envy neighbor Uriah his husbandly rights to such access. Nor, of course, would we expect a Biblical king from the fated House of Jesse to pity the woman that she must ordinarily sleep in an embrace unworthy of her beauty. In the complex grip of his lust, he did not intend to do anyone a favor.

The challenge was ultimately hierarchical. Surely the canniest of his subjects would note an incompleteness in his kingship as long as a junior officer was knocking off a niftier piece than the commander-in-chief. Over their dinner wine they would say comfortably, "Old David's got it all. But I don't know's I would trade places with him if I was getting what Uriah gets without hardly having to ask for it."

To strip such disloyal comfort from their minds would make

them better soldiers and subjects. Hence better men. Hence his scrotum drew taut around his stones, as once the pouch of his sling had tightened on the smooth pebbles from the famous brook in the Valley of Elah. He felt prepared to throw again as he had thrown into the forehead of Goliath. For the glory of the Living God.

He turned from the railing around the palace roof and beckoned a servant to carry a message to the Hittite's wife.

◈

See her with the king's eyes?

The effort of imagination is — almost — hopeless. Only the name of the Fair Bathsheba has outlasted the centuries she has been in the dust. But for us modern tourists in the hallways of the past, we sometimes come on intermediate images that incite us to go all the way.

Betsaba al bagno. See her live under the glazes of the baroque painters. Oh, tourist in the galleries of Florence or Venice, forbidden to touch even the frames of the paintings, with trailing wives, daughters, lovers eager to get back to the shops where Gucci gloves are sold — look! Here is a painting of Bathsheba with her big knees rocking, her head flung back a little to the tug of hair as the maid dries it, her eyelids down over some rollicking dream she might have shared with you when you were a boy as young as David beside his brook.

See her live in the lush Venetian pigment. Let pink be pink and white be white on the immortal titties. See how the painter has lavished his reds and oranges on the highlighted draperies and the jewels unclasped and laid aside in her wanton incarnation as *The Bather.* Note the dilation of leaves on flowering branches magnetized by the moment of her readiness, the ripples in the water murked by the sediment of her melancholy.

See how the painter's impudence mocked poor old David as a bearded Peeping Tom on a high rooftop, as far from this great cunt as you are, tourist. Hiding his hands under opulent robes, wearing a big turban to protect his middle-aged neck from drafts. Comedy and impudence have their place in the hindsight of art.

But David, in the moment of his kingship was no mere Peeping Tom. Fair Bathsheba found that out.

◈

Had he been deceived by seeing her at a distance? By tricks of atmosphere or his own capricious mood? There was no visible glamour in the woman who came in response to his summons and stood immobile in her plain robe. She was a housewife of Jerusalem, and among his tally of mistakes this threatened to be a whopper.

"You are the neighbor who keeps peacocks?"

He was going to complain that their barking kept him awake at night? No, no, no, no. He had nothing against peacocks.

She might have made some courteous reply, even to such a limp opening. But no. Her doves' eyes watched him without the faintest sign of comprehension. "I believe your husband, Uriah, is fighting in the front lines at Rabbah. Very big battle. Very important war."

That was his information. She found no reason to add to it. Wars were not in her line. The two of them faced each other uncomfortably like figures carved in a stone frieze. Outside the palace, beyond the colonnades, the landscape was still tawny with the lowering sun. Ravens flashed in the dark boughs of the cedars. Here in the king's cisternlike chamber there was a musty smell and an even, sultry gloom emanating from the stubborn woman.

It was a very good thing that the king had his harp in hand.

It gave him something to fidget with, and it might serve for more than that.

Broing. BROING! His twitching thumb swept the harp strings from left to right, tentatively at first, then with a ferocious imperative. Dance! Shake that thing!

From his very first wife, Michal, the king had been given to understand that foreplay was uncouth and unhygienic. A fastidious king would omit it. Since Michal was King Saul's daughter, he assumed she knew whereof she spoke. In any event, her successors had to follow her rules when Michal herself was shipped out. A little harping was all the foreplay they could expect. When he struck his chords in passion, they understood they were supposed to *hop to it.*

Not this hausfrau. She might have been tone deaf for all the appreciation she showed.

But the famous harp had a mind of its own today. It wanted action and would not be gainsaid. BROING! *BROING!*

The dummy stood like a tree in motionless air. And now the king leaned into his instrument and gave her the full orchestra. Plenty of percussion. Slurs and slavering discords. The ripped fragments of amorous melody. The thump of pursuit by roaring satyrs. The trilling of nymphs in wet spring woods, stumbling to be caught and ravished. Talk about your Rites of Spring . . . !

The result of so much erotic promotion was that he, not she, got steamier. Ten minutes . . . fifteen . . . of this assault by harp and she looked as frosty as before. But, if she had been a snake and someone had been there to hold its head . . . if she had been a cucumber and someone had offered to hold her vine, he would have climbed it now.

I am poured out like water, / and all my bones are out of joint: / my heart is like wax: / it is melted in the midst of my bowels.

Rapidly he was ceasing to be any kind of a king at all and was once again the lonely shepherd boy crooning to the stars. And that pitiable transformation at last got a rise out of her. She smiled and loosened the clutch on her robe. He could see just enough shoulder to recognize the skin he had seen from the roof.

"I am honored, milord."

"Yes?" he asked abjectly. "You are?"

"The maid told me you were watching from upstairs."

"The roof, actually. I was up there for a breath of air."

"Such a *warm* afternoon!"

A thrilling uncertainty swept him. The thumb of God plucked his entrails with as much fervor as he had given to his harp. The maid had told her! Told her afterward, perhaps, when the goods were wrapped up and taken back inside her little house at the foot of the garden. But . . . *perhaps* . . . just *possibly* the Nubian had whispered to her mistress while the show was still going on, and this vixen had submitted to the water play of the lubricious maid in an intentional display for his royal eyes.

It was just this possibility of slyness added to the innocence of happenstance that snared him hopelessly. He might never know the origin of her design on him. He could not ask (now or ever afterward) without stooping. He could not stoop without dimming the luster of the game they were to play with each other.

Bathsheba did not intend to bring him down from the heights of his power or passion either. She merely intended to be *honored* — her very word — by the uses to which he would put her.

Spastic from his toes to the royal nape of his neck, he raised his right arm commandingly to point at a spill of cushions on the floor.

With a sidling, deliberate step she went to them. "Here?" she asked demurely. She shed her robe and all trace of modesty with a single potent shrug. And there it was, neither snake nor cucumber, but the audacious womanflesh he had seen in the garden. With a sigh he moved to possess it.

Quicker than he, she was down on all fours before he could arrange her on the cushions, presenting to him her majestic rump. Like a . . . like a . . . like a sheep, though most miraculously transformed.

"No," he whispered with all the breath left in him. Because of his shepherd background he had rarely allowed himself to enter a woman in this fashion, and when it had happened, it was inevitably followed by accusatory dreams. His big brother, Eliab, and all the boys of Bethlehem circled him, scraping their fingers in a sign of shame.

"No!" he commanded. It was no use. A whirlwind from on high hurled him onto her. Into the mucid darkness where his kingly powers were melted by consuming fire.

Joab

◆

MANY YEARS later, because of what I had seen and knew from the old times, I expected Adonijah to fumble when he bid for the throne before King took his last breath. Because of Bathsheba's grip on King, I knew she would somehow wangle it for her boy Solomon instead. More is the pity, for Adonijah would have served us better, or almost any other prince. But knowing her, I expected the outcome to be as it had to be.

But do not write down I *predicted* Adonijah's failure. The difference between loudmouthed prophets and a soldier is I do not go around broadcasting what is sure to happen. It is often the worst possible tactic, and with Adonijah so certain he had everything sewed up, why should he believe me, had I warned him?

Joab, he would have said, what does Joab know about women? It is perfectly true I only knew Bathsheba from afar, and if I know what a gripper she must've been in bed, it is from pure military inference, at which I am very good. It is also common knowledge I have had only one wife at a time, up to the number of two, until this advanced age. A man has needs and there is nothing like a woman to take care of his needs. Beyond them two I did not need to venture, though in King's heyday there was a considerable amount of womanizing, following the example he set to us. It was sex, sex, sex, until every Hebrew whanger was an inch or two longer than they had been in holy times.

However, misdoubting my woman-knowledge is like deriding a general he doesn't mix it up in the front lines when there is a fray. Back in his tent, sipping pomegranate juice or pulling the bark off a twig, reading a report or two that is probably lies at best, what can he know how the battle is going?

I *thought* about Bathsheba is how I knew her and her wiles. Reasoning from grand old principles which are primer-simple, hence overlooked by those like Adonijah who think they are smart enough to take King's place.

Why did that woman never give King any more children after Solomon? His other wives dropped them thick as dewberries on a flood plain, and the concubines as well. We had so many princes in the prince season it's a wonder even go-getters like Absalom or Adonijah could stand out from the pack at all. And there is Bathsheba with her one and only son who does not look fit for the competition, though said to be wise.

What I mean is he didn't even have to be wise, with a mother like her to cut the mustard for him. She took her time to map it all out for him for when the right time would come, and in strategy you cannot have better than a good sense of timing.

Other wives came and went like it was a revolving door, and their litters with them, though always well provided. Some would point out that, as she hung on through good years and bad, Bathsheba got fat and dowdy. That's true as far as it matters. So they would point out she no longer had the clout with King a fresh young piece would have, be she only a concubine in rank, or that virgin laid on him near the end and said to be a real good friend of Adonijah's.

Little do they reckon what happens to an old man when some of his powers weaken parallel to the woman's losing her figure. King, she might say, do you remember the first time ever you nuzzled my coozie? And those poor old blinded eyes would wag open like he was beholding the Mount of Olives.

I could be wrong on details of how she could use the old clout in Solomon's behalf. I suppose memory is not a prime aphrodisiac, coming mixed with too much sorrow as it does.

Skip the details. Get back to principles always. She had borne him only one son to live, and that was because from before King even knew he would make it with her she had set her mind and woman equipment that Solomon would have the throne one day. I may not know much about the interior strings and levers and pulleys a woman has got up there, I only know they got them, and when employed in a disciplined manner, they can trap a lion or a tiger or haul Leviathan out of the deep, as the fellow says. Being King, King would think he had a choice in the matter of which son would succeed him, right up to his end, and for many reasons, he might have preferred Adonijah to that wimp Solomon.

He had no choice but what she gave him. Bathsheba.

Yet, it is true I came to Adonijah's "coronation festival" when he thought he had it sewed. It was a mighty occasion. There was to be *artistes* and acrobats from Nineveh. Tattooed men who swallowed fire. An Egyptian coon show with new-fangled instruments and belly dancers from up the Nile. They had done up the hall with plenty of brass pomegranates hanging from the balustrades, plenty of torches over the banquet tables, as well as ivory, apes, and peacocks galore.

You could say I attended on account of the acrobats promised. I like to see a nice somersault.

The crowd of ninnies that hang around a king was all assembled before ever I showed up. The feasting hadn't fully started, and Adonijah was hopping about, pink in the face, glad-handing one and all.

"Welcome aboard," he said when I walked in. There was so much whooping and inebriation in that big hall he must have thought I answered: "Glad to be here, your majesty." Like all the other guests would have said to him. They were there because they wanted to be counted for getting in early. That is the politician's vice. So you can claim later: Remember I was there at your feast when King David was still alive and hadn't yet declared himself for you. Some may even have come with rumors King was passed on, since he hadn't been seen out for a parade in considerable time.

If poor Adonijah could read lips, he would have made what I actually said to him closer to: "Don't count your chickens while Bathsheba can still lay an egg on you." (That wasn't my phrasing exactly. I think I may have said: "We'll hope for the best." Something neutral like that.)

◈

Altogether it was a fun party anyhow. I was stretching out my second cup of wine, watching an acrobat who could do a triple turn off his partner's shoulders, and enjoying the coon band.

Then there was this great big hush, in spite of the music going on. The acrobats was still twirling and the belly dancers grinding away, but all them wimp politicians was crowding toward the street door, and believe me their mouths had fallen open with no sound coming out.

There in the street was Solomon, sitting on top of King's

mule, waving his pudgy arm around so everyone can see he is
wearing King's big blue ring, which King must have given him.
Grinning — well, I won't say how Solomon was grinning at this
big joke, because, though I never liked him, I respect authority
and would not say dirty things about the anointed.

There, you bet, was Nathan the so-called prophet, beside him
to lead the mule in their procession. Out of sight to everyone
but me, but behind it all, as I knew in my bones, was the old
mutton herself. King liked to claim he invented the way to rule
these crazy people. Bathsheba invented how to be a Mother.

There before our eyes, Zadok wastes no time whipping out
the horn of oil he brought from the tabernacle. Just as quick,
there is Solomon off the mule and kneeling to be publicly
anointed. And poor dazed Adonijah had nothing for his trouble
but the bills to pay for the feasting.

The oil was very big with the crowd that Solomon, Nathan,
and Zadok had picked up along the way. HIP-HIP, GOD SAVE
KING SOLOMON. It all went so slick and neat you'd have
thought that most of it had been planned and practiced.

I knew better. It's the way people are, and Adonijah should
have known more about human nature before he tried to pre-
empt. Even poor Absalom had done it better.

The politicians who were still half drunk on Adonijah's best
wine took up with the others. The whole mob began to blow
on whatever would make a noise and clap their hands if they
had nothing else to beat on. Adonijah was grabbing at one or
another. "What does this mean?" Can you *believe* he kept on
saying that? No one bothered to tell him straight. I guess they
figured there was no use trying explanations for a loser who
couldn't grasp what had happened before his eyes.

Finally, as they are trooping back up toward the palace whooping and hollering that *Solomon sitteth on the throne* (though

he is having difficulty topping the mule, being a sorry horseman),
I noted Adonijah collaring the son of Abiathar, a sprout named
Jonathan with not much going for him besides the name, and
asking the same foolish question.

Jonathan spelled it out plain. "Verily our lord King David
hath made Solomon king. And the old king hath sent him with
Zadok the priest and Nathan the prophet and they have caused
him to ride upon the king's mule. This is the noise ye have
heard."

"Oh," said Adonijah. "Oh."

◈

So he turned to me. Where they always turned, him and his
father and his brothers, when they needed results. I am supposed
to get him out of this. If old Joab could spill Abner's bowels
in the dust (and don't forget Amasa, neither, when it comes to
big game), maybe I could get up to the palace and do likewise
for Solomon before he was set. King's boys go right to the finish
expecting a happy ending.

I gnawed the last shred of meat from the rib I was eating,
emptied my cup, and gave Adonijah a grin he first took to be
encouraging. Then I shook my head without a word.

Not that I would have minded taking Solomon out. But Solomon wouldn't have let me near him.

Then what should misfortunate Adonijah *do? Do* is a word
with a special attraction for those who can never make anything
come out right. When things go wrong, they chirp about *do*
this, *do* that, oh mercy, whatever can we *do* now?

"I would make a run for the temple," I told him. "Get inside
as fast as you can and grab ahold of the horns of the altar."

"Oh," he said and seemed to brighten. "Then what?"

"Then see what happens. Just grab the horns and keep holding on. You might also pray, if that is your inclination. It is a good place to pray."

"He won't kill me there?" Adonijah asked, his lip all trembling.

"I wouldn't bet on it," I said. Reflecting that King Solomon was wise. Had been raised that way by Nathan and his mother.

King David

———◆———

GUILT AND remorse and bad sheep dreams after that first copulation with Bathsheba. What was he thinking of? How could he take advantage of a soldier's absence at the front to top his wife?

The king is inclined to blame . . . his harp! This is not the first time the harp has got him into hot water. Scalding! But the harp is unpunishable and, furthermore, if it has plunged him into horrendous escapades, by the same token (with different melodies), it has always given him the way back to his duties and the satisfaction of kingly routines. In music, the heights and depths of errant mortality are reconciled beyond all understanding. Music alone among his counselors can promise consolation for the slimiest transgressions.

He is sorely tempted to blame the woman then. The old proverb has it that a fair woman without discretion is a gold ring in the nose of a swine. *Most* indiscreet of Bathsheba to bathe outdoors where an observer at a certain elevation could not help seeing her at her most enticing. Discretion would have led her to find some excuse for not coming up to the palace later. The wife of an absent soldier should, above all else, safeguard her husband's honor. Uriah would be well off without this present wife.

There is something even more serious to be laid to her charge, something bordering on witchcraft if you chose to give it its right name. What she did to her king's psychic defenses went beyond the crime of adultery. She had insinuated herself past his guard as if she knew full well how the most disastrous temptations lurk behind the sternest taboos. In his subsequent bad dreams, he saw she was indeed a female sheep with the satanic power of taking on the semblance of a lovely woman. A sheep in Lilith's clothing!

Now it was not his old companions of the sheep pasture who snickered at his violation of the taboo. It was a ghastly cherub of the Lord, ticking off the laws from Deuteronomy. Once he woke from a dream of being pelted with stones, crying, "I didn't do it! The dream was false. I never broke that law."

But even though waking permitted him to deny the fact, the cherub pursued him beyond the border of sleep, asking, WHO IS I?

In some high, starlit pasture on the mountain, a faceless child stumbled his way out of the flock with tears streaming hopelessly down his face.

Surely these dreams of abomination must have their roots in witchcraft. But King David reflects (wide awake and as rational as could be expected, given the impact of his experience) that King Saul never had any luck in trying to outlaw witchcraft. In truth Saul only mired himself more deeply in his troubles by recognizing witchcraft as a problem. A shrewd king will overlook the insoluble until it fades out of mind.

Also, the body has its mysteries no less profound than the

terrors of a wounded psyche. Now, wherever King David went, his nose twitched to an effluvium from his own pores, a scent persistent and sweet that could not be washed away or overlaid with coarser perfumes. Inhaling this joyful aroma, he knew his luck with Bathsheba was mixed, by no means all bad.

So he harped his way back to the mental health required to rule this headstrong, moody, murmuring race of his. Found a formula he could live with: SEX IS FUN. What a pussy! What a ride she gave her king!

◈

Guilt and remorse nevertheless. Beyond the inner crisis he was in serious default as monarch. *This was the time when kings go forth to battle.* It was still a few weeks short of full summer, when the battlefields would cease to be attractive and the troops would return to tend their harvests, orchards, and wives.

In the fine spring weather, files of his young men were leaping like goats from boulder to boulder down the stony draws to the plain before the city of his enemies. The glitter of armor flashed in lanes among the gray olive trees as the columns formed up. The carpenters were fitting rungs to the assault ladders before the walls of besieged Rabbah.

No reason for a still-robust king to miss a good fight. No good reason, that is. Yet he had sent Joab to lead the host this time, and the old bandit was doing a nice job of it, too. Already the children of Ammon had been pretty much wiped out. Rabbah would fall any time now. The scribes were already noting these circumstances in terms less than favorable to their king. *But David tarried still at Jerusalem.* Where would it lead when they began to footnote that cryptic detail or when gossip began to embroider it?

It was touch and go and a matter of timing before they began to say he stayed home because Jerusalem was full of wives overheated by the absence of their soldier husbands. Maids talk until they are shut up. Wives and concubines with too much time on their hands and too little action in their beds get very sensitive to new developments. There might have been a loitering witness who saw Bathsheba come into the palace that day and watched her go out, *after a certain length of time,* with such a wobble to her gait as would pretty well reveal how she had been honored by His Majesty.

While he reviewed these possibilities, his harp was mute. It sat in front of him in the armchair where he had parked it, for all the world like an examining magistrate, impartial but stern:

"As an old frontline fighter myself, I know the importance of homefront morale. I wanted the little woman to know her husband's valor had not escaped our notice.

"They get word to their husbands, you know. I wanted the little woman to tell him . . .

"I wanted the little woman to . . .

"The reason I did not go to Rabbah was . . .

"Don't leap to conclusions before you have all the facts, please!

"Let's be clear on one point. I answer only to the Lord.

"Let me make this very precise . . ."

The harp made no response to his eloquent defenses. Therefore he assumed they must be sufficient.

◈

But . . . Oh, my GAWD!

"My mistress is with child," the maid said. The same dark little bitch who had been whirling towels like a fan dancer's fans the day they seduced him on his rooftop while he was minding his own business.

Now her eyes and face were abased. To hide a grin? If he

whacked off her head then and there, would it still be grinning when it was swept off the floor?

King David uttered no comment. Was he supposed to offer congratulations?

But his harp began to sing from the armchair where he had placed it. First an almost hysterical little trill: How long has it been? How does she know it's me? Is she *sure?*

The king took the harp in his hands to mute it. "So?" he growled at the dusky maid. She trembled very appropriately.

"That is all. She sent me to tell you she is with child." The whisper was good and loud in this extraordinary silence, you bet.

When she was gone, the harp sang in full voice: Tell us again, O King, about the morale of the frontline troops. Tra la la la la. *Deliver my soul from the sword; my darling from the power of the dog. Save me from the lion's mouth; for thou hast heard me from the horns of unicorns.*

"I must think," he told the harp sternly.

NOooooooo! sang the harp. Too late for that. You must aaaaaaCT!

"I can see that," King David groaned.

◈

What he did might have worked. Not a bad scheme. Just what you or I might have thought of in his place.

And David sent to Joab, saying, Send me Uriah the Hittite. And Joab sent Uriah to David.

"Yes, I certainly envy you young fellows up there where the action is," the king said to Uriah, pacing energetically and sucking in his gut. With his mighty arm, he swung an imaginary sword and chopped with a battle-axe. Down went the ten thousands! The smell of heathen blood perfumed the desert air.

He could not have asked for a better audience. Uriah was an

eager beaver. He had grown to manhood fed on legends of his
king's prowess. What a treat to be personally called home and
addressed as a brother in arms.

Yet, Uriah could hardly believe he had come all this way for
a pep talk. (On the other hand, he showed no sign of expecting
anything more. To his sovereign, the Hittite appeared a young
man completely lacking in guile. A real patriot. He had the eyes
of a bee-stung horse, the rim of white above the pupil making
him look almost demented as he replied with rapid-fire vignettes
of swordplay at the edge of a wheatfield, the noisy arrival of
chariots when the issue of battle was in doubt, the shrill yipping
of Israel's pursuit when the dogs turned tail and raced back to
the cover of the city walls.)

"Wonderful! Oh, I wish I could have seen it. Marvelous! No
greater sight than seeing the back of your enemy. Ahem. The
only thing not clear to me is why — with you young men so full
of fire — is why General Joab hasn't cleaned up the mess by
now. Makes me wonder if he hasn't blundered a bit. If he was
up to snuff, you young chaps could be home now knocking some
little soldiers out of your wives, hey?"

A young man cannier than the Hittite would surely have
taken that bait. Concluded that he had been called home to
snitch on Joab. To guess his advantage now would be to toss in
a bad word about the brass. Not that there was a chance of his
replacing the battle-tested commander, but he might take one
more step up the ladder. Get a promotion on the spot for
whittling Joab down to size.

Not Uriah. Those jingo eyes never blinked. Joab was his
leader, and he would back him with his report as he did on the
noisy field. "It was the Lord's will," he said with perfect conviction. A short time back when they had seemed on the verge of
trapping the foe in the open, a storm with lightning and hail
and all manner of portentous crackles overhead had screened the

outmaneuvered adversary until he got back to Rabbah and dropped the gate.

"Tush," said the King. God was with Israel. Except in case of a heavy sin by . . . Well, no prophet was going to convince *him* that putting the wood to Bathsheba could produce lightning and hail so far from the pummeled cushions where it happened. Though, to tell the whole truth, he *had* heard some heavenly commotion when he fired the load into her.

"Just trying to see it clearly," King David said. "Joab is a mighty man and your trust in him confirms my confidence. Still, it's a pity you chaps can't come home to your wives and little ones. I sometimes think they're the real heroes of our campaigns. It's not easy to sleep alone when your loved one is far away."

Insincerity could not fully block the envious associations that rose around this theme. No doubt about it, this young Hittite was a handsome fellow if you didn't mind those fractious, unfocusing eyes. Arms all dusky gold from the battlefield sun. Torso clean-cut as a metal breastplate. Tippytoe stance, as if he were constantly ready to lunge.

And what a beard! No little tickler but a spiked flower of bronze within which the slobber of the warrior's excitement glittered like honey to attract a hummingbird.

"And there were a *thousand* of them when they came into the grove," Uriah remembered. "And we rose from our ambush like a flock of ravens. And they fought us there until all the leaves on the lower branches were red. And we drove them again into the city." He was up on the balls of his feet, reenacting the glorious shock of swords and javelins.

"Yes! And tomorrow you'll be back in the thick of it." The king was fully sympathetic. But what had to be done had to be done. The voice trained on psalms sank to a throaty vibrato. "But *tonight* . . . ! Ah, young fellow. My servants tell me you have a splendid wife right here in Jerusalem."

"We live just below the palace wall. You must have seen her."

"Unfortunately, I have not had the privilege. She must be delightful. And lonely, hey? I won't keep you from her any longer. You've told me what I wanted to know. Now scamper right out this side door and give her the best surprise of all."

"Sir?"

"Not a surprise? Ah, maybe you stopped there on your way to the palace."

"My orders were to come directly to you." For the first time Uriah's feelings were bruised.

"I see. Good man. Now hurry down and get the homecoming you deserve."

"O King, while the battle is undecided — friends, comrades right now trying to climb the bloody walls at Rabbah — it would be wrong to sleep with my wife. I must go back at once."

"I forbid it!"

"O King . . ."

"No arguments, please! Go back to the fight tomorrow with your valor whetted. Reminded of why you fight. Heh, heh. Reminded more than once if you hurry down home without any more silly argument." Not as a king but with fatherly warmth, he threw his arm around the steely shoulders and guided Uriah toward the side stairs. "Take an old soldier's advice. You know what I did the night before I slew my ten thousands? Aha, I thought you knew. Now hop to it. The battle won't be over before you get back."

As the hero at last reluctantly obeyed, the king had a further inspiration. His nose had caught the most seductive aroma coming up from the palace kitchen. He called the chef and made inquiry. The lamb? Most succulent tonight, milord. A tender creature that died under the butcher's knife with a smile of bliss, anticipating the pleasure it would yield. Which of the king's wives would share it tonight with his majesty? And the gravies?

Every wife and concubine on the premises had passed through his kitchen to sniff or stir the bubbling concoctions.

The chef was a eunuch, a man of forty with a splendid paunch to compensate for what else he had lost. His transferred sensuality was the flip side of a potential Casanova, never hard to decipher. What he could no longer do with his member, he did with his sauces.

"The lamb will do the trick," King David said. "You know the young fellow who just left me?"

"Him? The Hittite?" the eunuch asked. "I know him."

"And you know where he lives?"

The eunuch shrugged. His shoulders rose to eartop level. You bet he knew. Perhaps had long had his eye on one of Bathsheba's peacocks with a view to putting it on the royal table. Perhaps had already poached one or two. The king was in no position to criticize him for that.

To clinch the matter in hand, the king was inspired to send the best cut of the lamb, *plenty* of gravy, and a nice jug of bubbling red wine to the house of the Hittite forthwith.

"A hero," the king explained. "Tomorrow he goes back to fight our battles. Such stories he has told me! So tonight, while he is with his sweet wife, I want him to enjoy his deserts fully. If the lamb is as good as it smells, it is the least we can do for him."

The eunuch bowed and went out, humming under his breath.

◈

Done! Or as good as done. But if the king's design for covering his adulterous tracks has fallen into place so satisfactorily, why do we see Royal David up on the palace roof so late at night? The young moon is down in the west. The inscrutable constellations wink in heavens deceptively balmy and calm.

He has harp in hand. Is too dejected to try a melody. He is, in fact, afraid of what he might hear in the music welling from his canceled feelings. The harp might give voice to all those ifs and might-have-beens that he, as king, has been called to renounce. There are to be no escapades up in the ferns beside the hillside springs with the frolicking woman who might have been the bride of his younger days. Not even any casual wall-hopping into that little garden where the peacocks crouched all night under bushes heavy with blossoms. None of that. Let the unsung "Ballad of Bathsheba" be imprinted like a silent constellation up there where all impossible loves are printed and make no difference.

Yet he goes to lean on the parapet of the roof, exactly where he was on the day his enchantment began. Like an ordinary heartsick man leaning over a black cistern where the stars might be reflected on the musty water.

He sees no reflection. Nothing . . . unless there is some stir in the darkest corner of her garden, a scrabbling and a scampering with no discernible outline. Perhaps the heavy-bodied movement of a peacock going for its hen.

Irresistibly, his hand is drawn across his harp. BROING. Not loud this time. Not at all imperious. Only a little musical wail launched into the emptiness of the night as his nostrils twitch.

He imagines, nevertheless, that she hears it down in the bed of the room opening on the garden. He thinks she would lean up on her elbow when she hears. Shifting among the rumpled bedclothes and under the weight of the man snoring in satiety on the cushions of her breast. Smiling in pity at least for what might have been.

◈

Blear-eyed from the night's vigil, the king was out early, clacking his sandals down the palace steps on his way to the temple.

There were no religious consolations for what he had suffered, but going to temple would change the subject.

"What's that?" The king set his feet indignantly and threw up a stiff arm to point. "Who's that?" From what he had first taken to be a pile of laundry put down by a sloppy maid, two feet and a bronzed shin protruded. In King Saul's time, it was common to find beggars, sots, and even lepers to be shooed off the palace steps almost any morning. Things were ordered more neatly now.

"It's Uriah the Hittite," the king's bodyguard offered.

No doubt about it. That was a soldier's shin sticking out from the robe Uriah had pulled over his head and shoulders. A pussy-whipped soldier grabbing a last few winks before he hit the road. But on the spot to do his duty as the king might now command.

"He slept there all night," the bodyguard said.

"He . . . ?"

"He went not down to his wife."

Very irritating. The king went on to the temple wondering what he had tangled with now. A pint-sized Goliath with, alas, brains. Or maybe with even less brains than the unlucky giant. So little brains that the king's cleverness left him untouched, flying right over his head.

Uriah was awake when his king returned. The fellow sprang to attention, humming like a bowstring as David climbed the steps to deliver his mildest rebuke. With an arm around the hero's shoulders, breathing moistly into the closed, eager face, David said, "They tell me you slept all night on these hard stones. Well, that certainly convinces me you've got the right stuff. Even if you disobeyed my orders, I'm not going to be severe. But look at it this way. Does Joab sleep on the hard ground? Do I? We've got years of experience on you when it comes to soldiering. You can't do everything the hard way if you want to whip the Philistine."

In the second when Uriah was taking a deep breath to respond, the king worried what he might now hear was what he had actually and in fact done in Uriah's place. The passion in those fanatic eyes was that of a wronged husband, sure enough.

But the words that spilled now were rather those of a crazy prophet just in from months in the wilderness. *"The Ark, and Israel, and Judah, abide in tents; and my lord Joab, and the servants of my lord, are encamped in open fields; shall I then go into mine house, to eat and to drink, and to lie with my wife? as thou liveth, and as thy soul liveth, I will not do this thing."*

Outclassed by zeal, the king could think of nothing better than more bumbling condescension. "You bet. I certainly see your point. But now, after sleeping out here in a draft, you're more tired than yesterday. Do this, at least, my boy. At least go down and let your wife see you're in good shape. No scratches. Sit and have a talk with her today. I notice you've got some nice peacocks down there. A woman appreciates your helping her gather up the eggs. Or whatever you have to do with peacocks."

Now for the first time the weird eyes of the Hittite came into focus on the king as unbelief curdled into something close to contempt. Maybe it was true what they said about this king tarrying in Jerusalem. If he compared tending peacocks to rallying round the Ark, maybe it was a good thing he had turned command over to Joab.

Shaken, the king barked. "Report to the throne room at mid-afternoon." Let the cub make what he could of the angry and earthshaking tread of his retreating lord.

◈

The design was not past mending. This time the ploy was wine and a feast already spread in the throne room when the Hittite reported on command. Veils of incense wove over the raucous scene as the king drank and licked the gravy from the long bones of a heifer.

Shall even a most uncommon soldier not drink with his king?

Uriah drank. He was not used to drinking. The king had downed ten thousand cups in his time.

Then, among the silken wisps of smoke, the dancing girls came out. What applause they rated, these darting, shaking, leaping, laughing bundles of joy! How could the courtiers keep hands off such nubile goodies? They had license from the king himself to grab what they fancied and grab they did while the mirthful girls spraddled, threw back their heads, and kept the beat of the outrageous tambourines.

It was too much for the simple Hittite. At last, with a lewd shriek, he stumbled for the dark vixen who had shaken it in his face just long enough to light his torch, then spun toward a curtained alcove. Three sheets to the wind, the soldier followed her.

"Head him off," the king whispered. "Take him out and point him downhill toward his own house. Someone go with him. Make sure you get him inside the gate. Knock. Make sure his wife is there to handle the poor fellow."

❖

After one more night of agitation and hope, at last the king admitted defeat.

His courtiers told him, "The Hittite slept again on the palace steps."

So much for direct orders. Power is no better than the bunglers assigned to execute the sovereign will. Should he have ordered the dummies to open Uriah's britches and put it in her?

"Ink and a scroll," he demanded brusquely when he knew his

scheme was dead. He had the letter all composed when Uriah
was brought before him.

He had no pity for the hangover twitch in the young face. He
no longer tried to meet the far-focused eyes.

"Your wish is granted, soldier," he said. "It's back to the battle
for you. Without fail see that this letter is put directly into the
hands of Joab."

Joab

———◆———

I HAD TO laugh as soon as I read that letter with the hero standing right beside me in my tent. You can say it honed a better edge on my idea of what a king really has to be.

"Set ye Uriah in the forefront of the hottest battle, and retire ye from him, that he may be smitten, and die."

That's the message he had sent by Uriah's hand. In full. Took me a couple of minutes to read it and savor it.

Previous I had some trouble with "anointed." The king gets oiled by the priests, I thought, so that doesn't do anything to him. King Saul had been a chief and a fighter like my father as far as I could make out. Following them, I had refined many wiles for use on the enemy, since the ultimate weapon is always treachery, or surprise, as some call it. But the military mind doesn't rejoice in being oily.

I guess this gave me a new idea of how I would serve King. I lost some innocence right along with him to keep up. *"Set ye Uriah in the forefront . . ."* It was a riot. In a flash I saw how far King could go with me for the tail of his kite.

You note that at the time of reading I could not have known anything about King's hanky-panky with Bathsheba. Nor did folk back in Jerusalem see the picture until it was over and she was installed, so to speak, and even then there was nothing they could prove. That was his genius, to know just how close you could go to the cliff's edge while keeping perfect balance. From the letter, I got this flash of how the anointed mind could work, which is why I had to laugh as soon as I could take a breath. With the hero standing there at attention, mighty pleased with himself he had brought an important communication from King to his field commander.

I'll honor Uriah for that one-track mind. I always liked him. Wished I had a hundred of his sort. Never any question when you told him to do something, however risky. He'd just gulp air, stiffen up, and go for it. I mean he was a genuine hero, and I would not mock him for it but for the way things are.

He seemed — after all these years, I hold the picture of him very clear in mind's eye — a bit winded, as if he had run all the way from Jerusalem with the letter clutched in his hand, determined I should have it without delay. His chin stuck out like he was going to chop down the foe with that spiny beard on him.

"You have missed no action whilst away," I told him. He was relieved to hear it. "Get a good night's sleep. You look to need it. Your buddies are bivouacked up on yonder hill. I think they've got an ox on the spit. Maybe a skin of wine from the farmer. Bright and early tomorrow I got a mission for you. It will be a great day. By sundown we may be inside the city."

He nodded like I'd promised him a decoration, or just the wages we both agreed he deserved. A straightforward lad. No wink, no grin, just a military nod.

Then he says, "Will that be all, general?"

I could have laughed at the way he put it, but I said, sober as him, "That will be all."

◈

I have speculated sometimes since if the hero figured it out at the last minute, and just what he would have said when it dawned on him he was up on the city wall all alone.

For, as it actually turned out, he got up there in a nice piece of tactical assault. I supervised it myself. As action, it had my signature to it. I believe it could have worked as he thought it was supposed to. We had a noisy diversion going on a far corner of the wall. It looked like we had pulled the whole pack of them devils around to repel it. There was a mob of them kicking ladders away and rolling down stones onto us, such that Uriah and the dozen who had instructions from me were up their ladders and near the top before they were well noticed.

Then the hero took his mightiest lunge. He was on the wall, standing brave against the sky. You could see his teeth flash as he curled his arm to beckon the others over with him. He saw it was done according to plan.

Then he had to turn his attention to chop the defenders. It was mostly a bunch of screechy women and only two soldiers properly armed who opposed him, the women clawing and trying to grip his arms and legs until he sliced them loose, which he did nobly, and took the head right off one of the soldiers who stepped in. The other sort of fell back.

At this juncture, Uriah looked behind him again to see where was his support so he could race along the top of the wall to the gate.

Nobody there. His good buddies were back at the foot of their ladders, leaning on weapons, not stirring a muscle. They were first rate soldiers, too, who had their orders. But I don't doubt they all respected him and had shared ox meat and wine with him the night before. So he must have seen something grim and sad to their countenances. It wouldn't surprise me he was tempted to leap back down there amongst them, taking the chance of breaking his neck, because even him, he must have known something had gone wrong.

A hero is a hero. I didn't witness him hesitate a minute while whatever dawned on him that was going to dawn. He wheeled around to go it alone when the old spear went clean through him and he tumbled.

◈

Reporting mission accomplished to an anointed is often the trickiest part of the operation. Then is the time for them to boo-hoo and blame you for losses of citizenry. When King Saul was dead and had left the throne vacant, the officer who reported back to Jerusalem on it outsmarted himself radically. Damn fool had to garnish the report by adding he had given Saul the coup de grace on request. It was a fair bet, maybe, that King would be so tickled by his new opportunity he would pony up for assistance rendered. It goes to show that good bets are often one hundred per cent wrong.

How are the mighty fallen . . . You've heard the song King sang lamenting Saul and Jonathan. It became very popular. While the whippersnapper who brought the news had his body tossed to the jackals.

Very much the same case when I came back after knifing Abner. There was no doubt whatsoever I had nipped a dangerous plot and sent a message to other traitors they could not misunderstand. So King pissed all over me for services rendered. *Let it rest on the head of Joab* — and more lofty palaver about the lepers, cripples, beggars, and so on, I could expect in my family. Made my first wife so nervous she would not let me at her the rest of her days.

King went on and on as if he meant it. *"The Lord shall reward the doer of evil according to his wickedness"* was another way he put it. Meaning me, as the public had been coached to grasp. It goes with knifing a liked man, which no one could deny Abner was. Therein exactly was his danger. I liked him myself, for what that was worth.

King railed so against me at that time my own brother, Abishai, warned I had better go into hiding.

"No," I said. "A general must not expect to be widely loved. King knows he will need me for similar another day. I am like the butcher's dog. King will have need of me as long as he wants to be king. Long live the king."

You talk about downing Goliath with one stone. King was a born genius at knocking down two birds with one stone very often. And to bounce it off a third when his luck was best.

So this time I was not going to ride back myself to tell him of Uriah, nor put it in writing with my name on it.

I coached my messenger well. I rolled my eyes when he was supposed to roll his eyes at the awful tragedy. I blubbered where he was supposed to blubber for King, making sure the man knew how to lead in with plenty of detail, while he held back word Uriah was no more a problem.

"He will be very upset to hear the losses we have taken," I coached. "While he is taking on and plucking the harp most sadly, you blubber all the time. And also when he asks why we went too close to the city. Didn't we know they would shoot from the wall or the women throw down stones on us?"

"How could we fight'm we didn't get close?" the man asked.

"Stick to what I am telling you he will say. Otherwise . . ." I drew my finger across my throat. He savvied. He had heard about the Saul messenger.

"*Then* . . . then when he has told you what a poor general Joab is and how he should have come to take charge himself . . . *then* you say to him quietly, 'Uriah the Hittite is dead also.' Exactly those words I am telling you. 'Uriah the Hittite is dead also.' "

"What is that supposed to mean?" I wouldn't send an utter fool. He twigged this was some kind of code between me and King.

"You say it and see how he takes it. You are better off you don't know what it means."

Which he seemed to agree with as he made off down the Jerusalem road.

Nathan

———◆———

IN HIS special relationship with the Lord, nothing fretted our high-spirited king more than the Lord's whim of communicating sporadically through his prophets. Surely if Israel was as central to His design as common wisdom declared, He could have designated some low-ranked but literate cherub to get the signals through. That would have minimized confusion on most points.

Samuel had been bad enough. To this day, King David had still not puzzled out the old man's cryptic growls. In moments of doubt, he could still conjecture that Samuel had traded on the fear he himself inspired, mixing it inextricably with "fear of the Lord." After Samuel dismembered King Agag with Saul's sword, there was little doubt about the scope of Samuel's wrath. The irritability of an old man's constipation was hopelessly intermingled with the vengefulness of the Living God.

And now there was Nathan. A most untidy gaffer, trotting about in a soiled ephod, forever chewing the ends of his long hair, and blowing spittle when he came to deliver the Lord's rebukes.

This morning he had a dandy. The spittle was flying from his mouth like snowflakes in a blizzard.

"Lo!" He couldn't even manage a professional delivery for his "lo's." Maybe Israel was far down in cosmic rating after all, a fit subject for B pictures, indeed, if it could not field a more convincing prophet than this.

"Lo, there were two men in one city; the one rich, and the other poor. The rich man [What's he getting at with the italics?] *had exceeding many flocks and herds: But the poor man had nothing, save one little ewe lamb, which he had bought and nourished up: and it grew together with him; it did eat of his own meat, and drank of his own cup, and lay in his bosom, and was unto him as a daughter."*

"Stone him," King David said. "You know I'm sensitive on the poverty issue, Nathan, but the law makes no exceptions because of poverty or the sheep's age."

Nathan hardly paused. He had memorized the speech. *"And there came a traveler unto the rich man, and he spared to take of his own flock and of his own herd, to dress for the wayfaring man that was come unto him, but took the poor man's lamb, and dressed it for the man that was come to him."*

"I'll bet I know who it was."

Nathan wiped his mouth and hitched up his ephod.

"I've had my eye on him for quite a while," the king said. "Stingy is as stingy does. Cheats on his taxes, though we've never had any hard evidence to back it up. Well, evidence isn't everything, is it? If you say he took the poor man's animal for his own use, that's good enough for me. I'll fix his clock this time around. What's the matter, Nathan?"

Nathan was wagging his head. Not good enough.

"I mean the man shall surely die!" King David swore.

"Lo, you have misunderstood."

That was not hard where Nathan was concerned. If the Lord had to use him, He might have given him a semester of Remedial Hebrew.

"What else can we do? I see. We'll also seize his flocks and restore to the poor man four times what he lost in the transaction." When he wasn't actively prophesying, Nathan ran seminars on civil rights and the needs of the poor.

Then the hit came. *"Thou art the man!"* said Nathan. Well, he had practiced that one for sure.

"I am?"

Enough dodging. A prophet is a prophet, however dowdy, and now the sparring was over. The blow made the king's ears ring. In the tinny jangle he heard, unmistakably, the guttural of the cherub who had accused him in his dream. No use asking where prophets get their information. One way or another they hop onto the truth. Even a man's bad dreams aren't safe from their prying. Maybe this sputtering idiot didn't even quite grasp the full dimensions of his charge, but the Lord who had set him up for the parable knew whereof He spoke.

"Well. Maybe not *die.* That's pretty heavy for whatever was done with one little ewe. As I said, he'll have to pay back four for one. You heard me swear that. Four *prime* lambs. I don't care how scrawny the poor man's ewe might have been. Justice must be done."

Nathan and the Lord were not amused.

"You mean . . . ?" King David asked meekly.

"I mean."

"Uriah? And Bathsheba? I hadn't thought of matters in that way, to tell the truth. It just doesn't strike me that in her condition it's a good comparison to call her a *lamb.* A lamb, by definition . . . Never mind. I'm glad you brought the matter up with me, Nathan. I should have talked it over with you before I married her and put her in with the other wives. *The rich man had exceeding many flocks and herds.* That's clever, and I see now what you were driving at all the time. The fact is, I couldn't control my pity. I admit I'm soft-hearted. I realize I can't marry all the widows of my fallen heroes. But in this case, I had a weak spot for her husband, too. Champion lad! I'm told he was on top of the Rabbah wall all by himself when the misfortune oc-curred. But, as I wrote to Joab, *the sword devoureth one as well as another.* I had to put a good face on it for Joab. He was heart-broken, too, at losing one of his best men. When I heard the poor woman was with child, it seemed the least I could do . . . The husband would have wanted her provided for and . . ."

Nathan could not nail his king with fury the way old Samuel had. But puff him up with enough righteousness and Nathan gave a good imitation.

"*Your* child!" he bellowed. At least he stopped short of pre-dicting it would be born with four hoofs and a curly fleece. Thank God for the limits of human insight.

"*Thou art the man!*" There it came again, and the words had an unfortunately memorable ring to them. Let that saying get into the streets and the monarch was in for some nasty heckling.

"The fact that I married her . . ." King David began once more, fishing for a sincere way to end the sentence. No use. You can fool some of the people all of the time and most of them long enough to get around the corner with the loot. But how-ever the facts were come by, Nathan had the ones that counted.

"Yes, my child," the king said in contrition. Fairly caught, he was always sincerely contrite. Such sincerity was a major gift. He stiffened his shoulders to hear from Nathan what the Lord had in store for punishment.

"The child that is born unto thee shall surely die." Nathan got the sentence declared firmly enough. But then he had to wipe his eyes. Clearly it was not the punishment he would have thought of on his own, but he was, after all, only a messenger boy.

◈

Well . . . ! A sorry prospect. But not too bad. Not if he was to believe Nathan, and, thank God, God had no one else speaking for Him at this point in time.

Well, yes. If Bathsheba's child had to die to cancel the sin, that was a loss King David could bear.

If the Lord saw fit to settle for the misfortunate little babe, He might have had reasons He didn't share with old women like Nathan. A man of the world might still guess the babe in question was not King David's after all. That's what only the Lord would know for sure. Those peacocks in Bathsheba's garden weren't exactly watchdogs. Maybe some slacker had found his way past them and got in ahead of the king. You heard about that sort of thing with soldiers' wives. Yes, all things considered — and with a little harping to get them in perspective — the sentence was one King David could live with.

◈

Nevertheless, when the time came around and Bathsheba was delivered, the king's heart went out to the squawling infant. The baby was a husky, handsome little fellow. Maybe, somehow, out of human pity, he could smuggle the lad off to the hills around Bethlehem. Let him grow up, oh God, as a lusty shepherd boy, killing bears and wolves with a sling like his father before him. Let him perish, as I shall perish, for his own sins, I beseech thee, Lord!

But the Lord would not be gainsaid. On his second day of life the newborn child refused the nipple, and by nightfall everyone saw he would not survive.

No harping then. David beat his head on the stones of the floor. He terrified the palace guard by his weeping for seven days. When the child was gone, he rose up dry-eyed. *Seeing that the child was dead.*

"I shall go to him, but he shall not return to me," he said.

◈

Nathan gave a nice interpretation of the abruptly terminated show of grief. "So much else on our great king's mind," he told the wondering members of David's court. "So many of us who depend on him to solve the problems of our society."

One problem — about which Nathan never learned — was the knotting of a public relations lie to put the right complexion on the capture of Rabbah. In fact, Joab and his troopers had finally taken that stubborn city and heaped the streets with corpses. But, having done his part effectively, Joab wanted the credit for the victory to go where it would do the most good. He sent word that King David was to come at once, *"lest I take the city and it be called after my name."*

David got the point and acted on it. It is written that he *"gathered all the people together and went to Rabbah and fought against it and took it."* It's PR work of that kind that makes the Scripture what it is — not one lie in it, but just a little hard to puzzle out unless it's scrutinized with care.

Wasn't the king lucky to have a commander as self-effacing as Joab? Plus a new wife as yummy as Bathsheba? You bet he was eager to try his luck with her again and again, and soon she was once again pregnant. Legitimately this time. In these days, all things were coming to him at a cost he could live with quite comfortably.

Really at no cost whatever — except that he was being increasingly hemmed in by intimates who had his number. Nathan, for one, had pinched a ring in his nose. So had Joab. What about Bathsheba? Did she consolidate all her previous gains when he went in to comfort her for the loss of her first-born? Maybe, maybe not. At any rate, she popped him another son, and this one's name was called Solomon.

L'Enfance d'un Artiste

◆

NOT AN EFFEMINATE boy, you understand. The term lacks the requisite precision. It was only that from the first Solomon had a knack and a taste for the distaff side of palace life. A chip off the old block, right enough, but chipped from the sybaritic side of King David. Put a sling in this offspring's hand and he would have invented the brassière.

Far over in the Good Book you may read that Solomon grew wise from dialogue with many queens. The dialogue began early. He was only four when one of the royal concubines dragged him to his mother with the complaint that he had been "watching."

"He's just a child," Bathsheba said with some hauteur.

No argument about that. Nevertheless, the eyes the concubine had felt measuring her exposure were — how do you put this? — not exactly the eyes suitable for one so young. When she first realized she was being watched, something novel to her experience had made her well-oiled skin crawl.

"He asked me what they were *for*," the disoriented woman pleaded.

"He knows very well they are to feed little babies," Bathsheba said.

"I think he meant what else."

"Since you are childless, I suppose he meant your little boobies were good for nothing."

Solomon snickered. This gouging was what he really appreciated about women.

"Milord the king doesn't take that attitude. In case you were wondering where he's been the last few nights."

"Everyone knows he is in pursuit of the Philistines."

The ruffled concubine knew when to wind down an argument. With a last indignant huff at the smirking boy, she went back to finish her makeup.

Then Bathsheba most severely asked, "What *were* you doing in that unclean woman's chambers? I hope you didn't touch anything."

Without a blink, Solomon said, "Pursuing Philistines."

He was a wise child.

◈

After a few scrawny seasons, he got pudgy on confections the cooks prepared for the king's women. Before he reached puberty, his father worried over his weight problem. "People will say he looks like one of my eunuchs." All David's other sons traipsed the mountain trails and looked it. They were hard-handed from work with the threshers or from martial sports.

"Eunuch might be a good idea," Bathsheba said, for once despondent about her only child. "I've had complaints again."

"Ah, he's too young to do any real harm. The rascal likes to cuddle and always has. I notice him and you pretty well entangled now and then. Nothing wrong with a little touching."

"No, but he's been stealing their things. Perfume. Jewels. Girdles. I don't know what all. I know this for a fact. I've found some of the stuff in his room."

"Uh-oh. Have you talked to him about it?"

"Nathan has. I didn't know just what to say, though I'm the one who gets the complaints. And giggles, I might add."

"What does Nathan know about it? I meant it as a joke he looks like a eunuch. But leave it to Nathan and that's how it will end up. Solomon . . . *wears* these things he steals? And the perfume?"

"I don't think so. He told Nathan he did not wear them. No. It's something else."

"In God's name what?"

"He told Nathan he likes to put women in a snit. He said it puts them in a snit if they think he's got hold of their intimate things. I believe it's like some secret message he's sending them."

"All right at his age," the king said grimly. "But he should understand he'd better take it out of the palace once he's old enough to do any harm. Nathan may not have made that clear to him. Either you or I had better let him know I won't stand for it."

"You have a talk with him, then."

"Just give me some evidence to go on. About sending messages I couldn't care less."

◈

Nathan and Bathsheba had long ago taken over Solomon's education. That was why he grew up knowing nothing about right and wrong. The question Nathan always put was whether it was "wise" to choose one course rather than another. Cutting the ears off puppies, making fun of his father, overeating, tasting his own pee, misleading the blind, necromancing, playing with his weenie, driving mother birds off their eggs, wearing wool and linen together, practicing usury, liming the perches where the hunting falcons roosted, bearing false witness — such deeds were neither right nor wrong, but definitely unwise.

The whole swarm of King David's brawnier sons got a more conventional education. They danced, fornicated, and scuffled with godly zest in preparation for bloody adulthood; largely, no doubt, because they had been given to understand what was right and wrong and were prepared to fight over it.

But Nathan's inside track with Bathsheba opened the way for educational reforms that might have affected them all if they were not so plainly tailored to make Solomon the star pupil. He was quick to learn homilies about women, the poor, and various oppressed minorities. Proverbs dripped from his tongue almost from the time he began to speak. Parables with hidden snares gave him advantages over his more muscular siblings. He was rarely caught lying because his vocabulary glided through the truth with such intricacy that falsehood was unnecessary. He was tone deaf. Incapable of even the simplest melodies on the harp. But on the other hand, he had a nice gift for poetry and foreign tongues.

His younger brethren turned away from him because he was a sissy. The older ones ignored him. But Nathan comforted him with the example of Joseph, who had had his troubles as well with jealous brothers.

"*Behold, this dreamer cometh,*" Nathan said. "Remember that Ancestor Joseph bided his time until he was greater than any of them. Don't be sad if your brothers go their coarse ways without you. One day you will outshine them all."

The encouragement was beside the point for a boy whose mother had convinced him he *already* outshone them.

◈

What Solomon was prepared for by his progressive education revealed itself soon after his twelfth birthday. After puberty the childish disguises peeled away and those with eyes to see beheld the future monarch.

What had been gross pudginess smoothed down within a year to a rotund but not at all unmanly sleekness. No muscular bulge disturbed the pure, full curves of his shoulders, arms, or legs. His first little beard came in like an adornment of ebony from Egypt. The limpid, dark eyes (his mother's, exactly) lost their unnerving slyness. If he had secretly experimented in wearing the clothes he snitched from palace women, the experiments taught him how to wear the garments of a prince with suavity and winning grace. The smooth indolence of his gestures no longer seemed effete but, already, regal. He wore no jewels on his dimpled hands. His smoothly tapered fingers and exquisite nails required no enhancement.

Now it was not he who ogled the harem. The women of all ages watched and sighed over him. Notes were passed. Assignations hinted. Graffiti in feminine handwriting had to be sanded from the cubicles in the woman's bath.

Yet this ambience of all-enveloping flirtation remained innocent — in a manner of speaking. There were no overt trespasses. His father was as sure of that as he was sure that some kind of sorcery was afoot.

Shrewdly suspecting that if anyone knew how Solomon managed to focus so much latent eroticism it would be his mother, King David went to the source.

"It's the amenities," Bathsheba said. "Solomon understands the importance of amenities in a woman's heart. A little token for their anniversaries. Do you remember that? Some small gift for no reason at all. Flowers for this person or that. A trinket here and there does wonders. You think all we wives want is semen, semen, semen, and always huffing and puffing over us, ha!"

Watch out for her when she speaks of "we wives." Bathsheba's usual term for the others was "those women."

This was a time when she had almost stopped putting out for him. Taking the hint from his conversation with her, he procured a fancy negligee from a Syrian trader. A little more than a trinket. Guaranteed to make the woman thankful, the trader said.

It didn't fit. It was the wrong color. Her headaches were as frequent as before. "Try harder understanding the other person's point of view. We wives are persons in our own right. Respect our personhood! You never think of but that one thing."

Stubbornly he answered, "That's right. Pick it and peel it, wrap it up and tie it with a bow, it always comes down to that one thing in the end, and you know it. Back to the matter of your boy, Solomon, there's more to it than just his remembering anniversaries."

"True," Bathsheba said. "Now you are catching on to what women want. It is certainly not raw sex. That's insulting. What Solomon understands is courtship."

"Who's he been courting, tell me?"

"For its own sake. It's an art, which he is inclined to by his nature. We call it courtly love."

"You and he have *given it a name?* You call it 'courtly love' now?"

"Persons who are attuned to it call it that name, yes."

A catchy term, and at least it distinguished Solomon's peculiar gambit from anything his father was used to. The idea of "courtly love" at least helped him categorize and study the frequent little snatches of amorous song that came to his ears these days. Of course, not from the boy himself. He couldn't carry a tune in a bushel basket. It seemed to be the younger concubines and maids who could not keep a lid on the longings the unique prince roused in their bosoms. Tra la la la la. *La la.* Different notes and voices. Same theme. Not even the name of Solomon surfaced in these yearning lilts. The listener felt the eroticism they expressed was not to be fulfilled by kisses, caresses, or more emphatic contact. You could call it ethereal, except that the theme was so purely sprung from desires of the flesh. An endless, intermittent flame in the air. Disembodied diddling. *Coitus interruptus* carried over from previous incarnations.

Bullshit. A king who needed to keep his feet on the ground could not be satisfied with such wispy conceits. "The boy pulls his pud all the time and it's got out of hand," he charged Nathan. "You seem to be responsible for shaping him up. You've got to do something about it. Has he ever been laid that you know of?"

Nathan hopped from foot to foot. "So young? So well brought up? He should go with the strange woman? There was a certain man who had in his flock many young sheep. And one young ram with curling horns and curly fleece stood apart from all the rest. And lo, the man looked on the fairest of his lambs and said I will sacrifice him . . ."

"I don't want to sacrifice him. I want him laid like a normal boy his age. Shucking his nubbin will rot his brains, which is about all he's got anyhow."

Nathan folded his arms and closed his eyes in refusal. Autoeroticism was unwise, beyond argument, but he had never caught the prince at it, and if he had, he would be no party to a crude remedy.

King David gave up in bafflement. If the boy was addicted to beating off because he thought he was too good to lay it out like a man, that still explained only half the strange phenomenon.

How did the women know, and what did it matter to them if

royal semen was being spilled in their name or in their direction? What kind of eerie messages had Bathsheba's child learned to convey to womanhood at large? If this was what they called courtly love, was it going to be the plague the Lord laid on the next generation?

Suppose that by some fluke Solomon became king someday. He would rule the female half of the kingdom very well, it looked like. Talk about charisma. The boy had mastered it absolutely if all he had to rule was women. Keep them wanting. That would take care of one half of politics.

But dammit, there were always Philistines to fight, not to mention powers of uncertain loyalty closer to home.

◈

Therefore the king tried to ignore the Solomon problem, placing his hopes in sons more like himself.

Absalom's Revolt

Solomon

---◆---

I WONDER WHAT Brother Amnon did with Sister Tamar.

I asked Bathsheba what it was and she said she didn't know.
I don't believe her. She finds out everything that goes on in the
family down through the cousins. That's why the other women
are afraid of her. I don't know how she does it, or I would do
it, too.

I asked Nathan. He said what Amnon did was not wise. It
was *very, very, very* unwise.

So I think I know.

I will shut the door and pull the covers over my head and
make a long poem about it.

Joab

———◆———

I HEARD IT from all sides that Absalom was the one to watch, both on his own merits and how King favored him. The only time the fag Achitophel ever sought me out it was to sound me would I like to see Absalom someday on the throne.

"That is looking a long way ahead," I told him.

A fag politician is a politician in spades, and Achitophel knew the drill as well as any I have watched operate. "Many, many years," he agreed, sweet as honey. "We old-timers who remember the disorder after Saul's death might feel it is never too soon to plan for an orderly transfer of power. If we look at the precedents in other countries, we'll see the merit in an early designation of the heir apparent."

"Other countries have not got the Living God to sort things out for them."

"Well said! In all my traveling I have never found a kingdom so blessed as ours. Yet sometimes I grieve, as you must, at our capacity for dissension, even in times of mortal stress."

"What do you want me to do?" I asked shortly, not needing from him sermons on patriotism.

"Since you seem to agree that Absalom has the potential to be as perfect as his father, and since your influence with the king is legendary, and since Absalom himself respects you so highly . . ."

"He would make it worth my while if I spoke for him now?"

Achitophel never blinked at that. A diplomat will weave your language into his without a pause for breath. "Absalom is a generous youth," he said. "Headstrong but generous." Achitophel had arrived at my place a living advertisement of what generosity will do for you if you can wangle it. Big gold chariot pulled by spanking bays. A big jeweled belt and several gold chains hanging down his bosom, so my old lady had curtsied to him when he came in, as she can't help doing with the prosperous. The perfume he had on his handkerchief smelled more like money than like any natural flowers.

"I don't expect a commitment from you," he said. He kept looking deep in my eyes whilst he was hinting bribes. Faggots aren't brave, they are just confident a man won't hurt them. I have to say his charm worked on me. Another person making such an offer I might have tossed bodily over the wall.

"Don't expect it now or ever," I said. "And there is one other thing you should know. I don't have influence with King."

He refused to believe it. Naturally thought I was being modest and admired my modesty as a political trick.

So I am one step ahead of him in strategy. The precise truth is I wouldn't *use* influence on King, because too often I have seen how any stimulus whatsoever *over*stimulates him.

I try to keep his feelings throttled down while time ripens what has to be.

◈

By experience I am mistrustful of details. So in the mess over
Absalom's sister Tamar I never sought them. My point would
be chiefly that in matters of rape the testimony never will be
clear. You say he forced you? Sure Amnon is bigger and stronger
than you, but did it occur to you to yell for help? Well, if I
yelled for help before he put it in me, he hasn't done anything,
and I have cried wolf. Afterward what is the point in crying for
help? Mend as best you can. And Tamar did well in asking
Amnon to keep her on after the dirty deed. What kind of bastard
would add insult to injury by putting her little ass in the street
again when he had had the use of it? Amnon. He did it. Which
insult on top of injury was what broke the camel's back for
Absalom. You see how the shit flies in all directions once it hits
the fan?

No maidenhead was ever glued back together by calling for
justice. The matter will naturally be settled by parties who have
the strongest feelings about it. Since Tamar had a brother, namely
Absalom, to cut down the rapist for her, my position was only
he did the natural thing, and I would gather up the pieces from
there on as best I might.

I had to take care of King's interest above all. By now, I was
well versed in what would satisfy him. You take what he *says*
he wants, multiply by three and subtract seven, divide by eight,
add an apple and two peaches, then figure what would be to his
advantage in the long run and do it for him.

Admitting I lacked finesse in getting Abner off the scene, I
could recall I did just about right for Uriah. When the dust
settled, there was nothing left for King to do but plough into
his new piece with her champion ass and big brown eyes.

I understand she still gets mournful when she refers to "my
first husband." How's that for orchestration?

King likes some theater, even when it is only killing time, so
I resolved once again to coach someone how to lay out the con-

siderations about Absalom, now that he had killed Amnon and fled the country. I got this wise woman of Tekoah and here is the act I drilled her in:

"Help, O King!" (Not a fancy speech, but it gets things going.)

She gets the royal nod. "That's what I'm all about. To assist the afflicted, however lowly."

"I'm but a poor widow." (We dressed her shabby to make sure he understood she was a widow-type widow and not there hoping to go the Bathsheba route with him.)

More royal nodding. Widows and orphans a specialty.

"Thy handmaid had two sons. They were fighting together in the field with nobody there to part them. One smote the other and slew him." (Never mind that in fact Absalom had his servants get Amnon drunk and then jump him, ten on one, while Absalom was already saddling his mule to get away from the scene of the crime. A little editing is necessary for good theater.)

By about this point, I calculated, King would see the parallel to his own family problem and sniff that he is being offered a way to do what he has wanted all along, favoring Absalom in his heart as he does. Great — as long as he can lay it on a widow woman for putting the idea in his head.

Then the widow wraps it up with a little improvisation so he can't play dumb later, change his mind, and claim he has to judge each case on its merits, her trouble having nothing to do with Absalom and Amnon, he not being a widow with no more sons lingering about to fill in if Absalom stays permanently over in Geshur.

She could say: *"Thou wouldest not suffer the revengers of blood to destroy any more lest they destroy Absalom"* . . . Woops, when the point is clear enough anyway, make that "my son" instead of "Absalom."

Then King can say, as if inspiration had suddenly dawned:

"As the Lord liveth, there shall not one hair of thy son fall to earth."

◈

So King had his theater, and when the lights came up again he's grinning like a Chessy as he says to the so-called widow, "Joab put you up to this, didn't he?"

Not saying it to credit me but to milk a little flattery from the woman. "Oh, milord is wise," she said. Couldn't hide a thing from him. The wisdom of an angel of God. That sort of thing.

Fair enough. The flattery put a head on what we started rolling with our act. Settled King in the right mood so he sent word to me to fetch Absalom home from exile.

◈

Everything forgiven? No sir. In all good faith, bushy and bright-eyed, the boy came back to Jerusalem ready to boohoo along with Dad about poor Amnon and poor Tamar and anyone else who counted that had got hurt.

King wouldn't let him near the palace.

"You can't have everything," I said to Absalom. "Give it time."

"How much time?"

"The time it takes," I said. I wanted him to know this was my very best advice, and what I had done for him so far should be warrant I was worth listening to.

It never is when people have got impatient blood in them. Instead of heeding, the boy takes up again with Achitophel, who had washed his hands, but clean, whilst the scandal was worst.

Achitophel was almost my match for strategy, I will say that. Month after month, he did nothing for the lad but sweet-talk him with promises whilst waving that perfumed hanky in his face to hypnotize him along.

Myself, I had about written him off. If someone wants to depend on me, let it be whole hog or none. My counsel would no more mix with the faggot's than oil and water.

So what does Absalom do to get me going again? It being Absalom, he sent his servants to fire my barley field. The fire might have taken the buildings if the wind had been right.

Into all the smoke and flame he came striding — bold as brass, I will say for him. "Turn a hand," I shouted. Without ado he whipped off his best cloak and beat at the flames like a soldier. It did me good to see him not afraid to advance right into the fire. I laid back and let him finish before it took the last acre.

"You are acting like a spoiled brat for sure," I told him when he approached, rubbing the black off his face. His big head of hair had taken some singeing, too. I guess he saw in my face I was not altogether mad. We have had too much peace lately. "Why'd you do an asshole trick like this, asshole?"

"I had to get your attention," he said, most grim and fierce. "I want everything settled."

"It's settling."

"Now!" he said. It wasn't a worked-up or artificial kind of bravery. Somehow he had become a real man over in Geshur. "Go to my father and tell him I have to meet him face to face. If I am guilty for executing the rapist, let my father kill me on the spot. If I'm justified, I want a clean pardon. He's got to make up his mind, and he can't put it off anymore."

"He's made up his mind," I said. "You'll do, boy. But you owe me for my barley."

David

◆

"YOUR SON HAS a child of his own now," the visitor from Geshur tells the king.

"Ah?" All mention of Absalom has been discouraged in the palace for what seems like years.

The unwarned stranger goes on. "A little daughter."

"Oh. A girl."

"He has called her name Tamar, after your daughter. She is a healthy, happy child. She has already taken her first steps. My wife and I . . . I have said something to offend you?" The visitor springs up in alarm, bows, and remains frozen in a posture of consternation.

"I am not well today," the king says. He has a fierce grip on the two carved arms of his throne. He is trying to haul himself upright. His eyes burn like coals in a blacksmith's forge. "Nothing," he says. "It is nothing. Please express my friendship to your king Talmai when you return. It is nothing. Nothing."

"Milord . . ."

"Her name is Tamar?"

"Tamar."

◈

He is riding alone by night in a black desert storm. The king has outdistanced all the fleet horsemen of his army. The bitter sting of sand blown against his face goads him to greater and greater speed, but never enough. Frantically, he spurs the bleeding flanks of his horse while the wind tears at his cloak.

A child is clinging to his saddlebows. Over the wind he hears the whimper of her sobs. "Don't be afraid," he says. "They'll never catch us now."

The sobbing stops. There is no wind. No stars. No child. Only himself astride a horse mortally stricken by the wild gallop.

I lost her. And my boys.

◈

My son, had you met him in the field, brother against brother, though he was dangerously armed and you were naked, you might have slain him for the great wrong he did our Tamar. But we do not deliver our blood to the hands of servants. You killed him by strategy when he was at your mercy. You set your servants on him like a pack of dogs.

Yet the king would have forgiven Absalom the vile perversion of justice — if he had been granted the power to forgive faults past retrieving. The wish to forgive is coupled hideously with the impotent wish to change the past. There is a mighty wall excluding him from the kingdom of what might have been, confining him to the prison of what was and shall be.

If I had taken Amnon's life with my own hand when I knew the crime he had done . . .

*Nor have you the power to forgive me that I held back when
I should have acted, Absalom.*

❖

He is going down one of the back stairways of the palace when
he hears a child crying behind a closed oak door. Even as he
passes, the door opens on the dark room and his wife, Eglah,
slips out.

"Is the child sick? In pain?"

She smiles at his anxiety. "It is nothing. Your son is afraid of
the dark."

"Then give him the light he wants."

Eglah shakes her head, dubious but firm. "A son of David
must not be a coward. He will outgrow it. I have sat with him
an hour in the dark. Soon he will cry himself to sleep."

"He will outgrow it," the king agrees. "But *now* he is afraid."
Men can face the assault of years. It is the terrible present moment that overcomes them.

Eglah would like to please her lord, but he has confused her
about what he really requires of the mothers of his sons. Confusion makes her unrelenting. There will be no lamp this night
for the boy who has looked upon the face of darkness.

The king remembers that Absalom, once upon a time, was
afraid of the dark and seemed to outgrow that fear along with
others.

❖

Across the floor of the throne room comes Absalom with a
bright sword held flat across the palms of his two hands. He
comes with a confident step, as if the sword were a gift his father
is sure to welcome. He cannot see the dark figure that walks
behind him, matching him step for step, empty-handed, implacable.

The king will not touch the sword offered thus and Absalom will not keep it. After an awkward moment it clatters down on the stone floor, and Absalom is robbed of the ceremony of reconciliation.

His father only says, "You have come home."

Two men of equal height embrace. At last there is a quaver in the father's voice. "They tell me you have a child of your own now."

"In Geshur."

"You left her to grow up in Geshur with her mother? Yes. All right. She may be happier in another kingdom."

Neither man dares utter the lost child's name.

"She will be fair," says Absalom.

Joab

———◆———

YOU KNOW WHAT? He paid me for that barley, too. Every shekel it was worth without me having to mention it again when King had taken him back.

Absalom was minding his p's and q's and setting great store by reputation since the time he had to think things over in Geshur. Not that he wasn't well liked in town and with a special variety of reputation before the trouble, which had now come to a happy ending.

Before, he had him a reputation for being flamboyant and a champion cocksman with the maidens. He was admired, and you asked people what they admired him for they would get a silly look and say it was for his *hair*.

Indeed it was quite a head he had on him, kind of freakish, and once a year he would get it cut and *weighed*. It became a fad for kids his age to gather round while the barber was at him and guess how heavy it had grown since the last time. The year it went over two hundred shekels king's weight, there was talk of hardly anything else among the kids. Even my nephews, Abishai's punks, were trying various oils on their heads to make it look frizzy like Absalom's. It wasn't until the Tamar scandal and prophets pointing out how funny fads somehow brought on rape and murder that you saw any good grooming reappear again.

We even had trouble with it in the army until I threatened to take on haircutting myself and the recruits knew I meant to take it off *at shoulder level* from the top down.

In his wild days, the bushy hair had sort of stood for all the ways he had of driving maidens off their gourd. Then it was a sight to see the boy come lickety-split in his chariot down the main street. At a given moment he would hit the reins so wheels and hoofs screeched wild on the paving. And there in the cloud of dust he has raised would be a maiden with big round eyes, wondering what all the noise is about.

She is what all the noise is about, of course. What she sees first, leaning his curls over the side of the chariot, handsome like some heathen god with all his teeth ashine, is this prince of the House of David. All of a tizzy she clutches herself up and says on the order of "My, you took my breath out of me, I thought it was a runaway." What she is really thinking is that he is fixing to leap on her and shame her in public view.

Given his modus of operandi and his luck, rape was never necessary, as it was for Amnon. "It was the horses' idea," Absalom would say. "These are seeing-eye stallions I got hitched up today. They spotted you from as soon as we turned the corner. I couldn't control them when they beheld your luscious form."

"There is no such thing . . ."

"You bet there is. Now I know how right they were."

". . . as a seeing-eye horse."

"You think not? You hop right in the chariot with me, and

we'll canter around while we test their powers. Whatever you hanker for they will likely spot it and bring you right to it."

"I was on my way to the well," the maiden would say (or to the temple, or to visit Aunt Rebecca, or to watch the caravan come in from Tyre; you name it).

"Then put your jug in my chariot," Absalom said. "I know a spot not halfway up the mountain where you can get water so fresh it makes your teeth curl."

"No such water," the maiden says. But by then he has already got a purchase on her jug handle, and if the horses aren't exactly seeing-eye stallions, they know what he has in mind and are on their way, the maiden hanging on to the chariot sides with both hands while everything else on her bounces like oranges in a sack about to bust open.

With my own eyes I had seen him a few times come back from one of these little excursions, and the way his ponies came back prancing you might have thought it was share and share alike with them. The maiden would have her face covered as she dangled her feet from behind the chariot, but peeping out as if she didn't really mind being noticed with such a popular prince. She would likely come back with her jug full of water, too, to show Absalom kept his promises.

It is funny how the wilder the boy the more sensitive he will be about his sister's honor.

◈

All changed when he came home from exile to be once more Number One prince.

But character don't change, neither his nor the public's. Character is like water: you block it one way, it will feel around the obstacle and come out somewhere else flowing in the same direction. In their thirst, the public was waiting for the old Absalom to show again and keep them entertained in the slack times of peace that had come on us. We were all missing war for its own sake, and being the people we are, it was always in everyone's mind that the goyim were still out there beyond the hills, breeding like rabbits against us. And who ever knew what else they were cooking when we weren't fighting them, pre-emptive or otherwise?

Now that the young were jaded with sex novelties and also warned off them by the example of Amnon being held up to them, the fad swung to athletics, where Absalom also excelled and became a leader. Now instead of charioting around with only a plump girl to give his team something to pull on, he would have as many as fifty, a hundred young fellows running alongside, dancing and singing and shaking sticks. On their way to games outside the city wall with much throwing and wrestling. Absalom set many records, which stand to this day.

I marked it was not just young folks who thought him their natural leader. A lot of silly elders could be seen lifting weights or running round and round the palace gardens with nowhere to go to. Women who used to lie about their age would brag on it now as they kept their bellies flat by funny dances and exercise. They would not admit their age, you see; the notion was that they would always be young in spite of years. From that, like water finding its way downhill, the talk began that what was needed was "youthful leadership" and "vigor" in the kingdom, with a side to it of disparagement of King for not being the curly-headed young fellow who had been an improvement on King Saul.

◈

Whoever seduces who? That is the riddle. Was it those maidens wagging their fat down main street in all innocence who used to

seduce Absalom in his boisterous days? Even poor Tamar se-
ducing Amnon with a view to marriage, which he wouldn't give
her? Arguments can be made.

It can be argued it was the public seduced Absalom as much
as him them, and I doubt in the beginning at least he had a design to revolt against King until maybe Achitophel drew a
picture for him and said that's where it had all been leading.

Whenever you lack war, you get tourism and business travel.
A lot of hankering folks coming into the capital with their own
interests on their mind. There was a felt need for someone to
listen to all the avarice and discontent they brought with them.
And good-looking, warm-hearted Absalom, he fell into the slot
of taking serious all their pissing and moaning. It got so almost
any morning you would see him, neatly combed and business-
like in garment, sitting out front of the palace sociable with
all comers.

"Hell-oh!" says Absalom. "Why that's Ma and Pa and I see
you brought Grandpa to town with you today. And these handsome little shavers are *all* yours? You must be very proud they
all turned out so fine. First time in Jerusalem? The bazaars are
right down that way, and when you've done your shopping, you
maybe will want a little kosher snack. If you're tired of mutton,
I can tell you just the place to go. If Grandpa wants to stretch
out a while in the shade, you can bring him around to the back
end of the palace gardens. If the guards try to keep you out, say
Absalom sent you . . ."

In business or a legal matter they brought in, he would jot
down the figures and worry over them like it was his own
money at stake. "Oh my!" he would moan. "Oh dear me! You
say you've been owed since last summer? Three sheep and a
used tent? I'm sorry to tell you, friend, that your chances of
collecting are very dim. As things have gone we've got a lot of

corrupt and lazy judges in the kingdom. Too long in office, people say. I know of some myself who could hardly be bothered about three sheep and a practically new tent."

He'd put his hand on the fellow's shoulder and say, "Oh! *oh, that I were made judge in the land, that every man which hath any suit or cause might come unto me, and I would do him justice."*

I'll tell you this — I think he purely meant what he said. He was a genuine idealist, Absalom. He couldn't listen to a pack of greedy lies without wishing to do something to help everyone. He itched for power because you can't do much good without it.

But from things as they transpired, I would not say he just hoped to be appointed local judge.

Solomon

———◆———

I HEARD BATHSHEBA put Father through the jumps again.

She said, "I'm warning you, David, watch out for him."

"Which one?" he asked with a mournful little laugh. He has an expressive voice.

"You have a point there," she said. "It's hard to find anyone to trust these days."

"It's only that I'm tired," he said. "Tired and old. Maybe it's time I let someone else take over, after all."

"David! You're not a bit old. Tired maybe. Old never. Do I make you feel old?"

"Well . . ."

"Poor ittums. He doesn't feel old to me. Not a bit old."

I heard them moving around. First Father's sandals sliding on the floor, then his bare feet whooshing. Bathsheba's slippers whispering a kind of dance.

"No," she said. "I only meant you haven't got a thing to

worry about if you'll just keep an eye on Absalom. I'm sure he's a well-meaning boy. When he came back to us from Geshur, I thought he'd turned over a new leaf. I was worried when he used to hang around with that pansy Achitophel."

Father's laugh sounded exasperated now. "That's the last thing I ever worried about in Absalom's case."

"I didn't mean Achitophel would get to him. Achitophel has foreign connections and you know it. If I were you, I'd have had spies on him since he was in Damascus. But now the boy's just as thick with Joab as he used to be with Achitophel."

"With all your spies, I don't need any."

"You know what I think of Joab."

"I can't trust anyone but you," Father said. I think he meant it for a joke, though it sounded pitifully flat. I heard his bare feet shuffling again and the sound of a slap. The slap sounded like a joke, too, and she said, "David! I can't even say you're not old without giving you a *boy's* ideas."

"Come on. I've respected your personhood for three months now."

"That's not very funny! It's not funny at all. You know I'm sensitive I've put on weight. I'm the one who's getting old. I wish I could be your own Bathsheba again."

"Bah," he said. "The more Bathsheba the better."

"David!" she said.

"It's no use. Personhood or not, I'm going to."

"Bah," she said — though it sounded more like baaaaaaaa!

Then they were going to it like a storm right on the bed I was hiding under. I kept laughing until they were finished and she said again, "I'm warning you to keep an eye on Absalom."

"I will," he said.

I will have to try respecting personhood.

Joab

◆

"MARCH WITH a following wind," I told Absalom the first afternoon he took instruction from me in my back yard.

Very earnestly the young fellow asked did I mean that literally.

"Don't ask for explanations of prime principles. To understand them you have got to meditate them long and hard as well as make split-second recognitions when they apply and when they do not."

He shook his bushy head with a game grin. "I see," he said. "I see."

"The prime principles are: March with a following wind. Achieve the high ground. Never be stupider than you've got to be. Don't make mistakes."

"Is that all?"

"Now you can turn my grindstone for me while you meditate."

Reading a man's face while he watches the edge of a blade grow finer on the stone tells me much of what I need to know.

I was satisfied with what I saw on his, watching from the corner of my eye.

I was not dismayed he did not return then for some weeks. Only my old lady and grandson were put out. They had taken an instant liking to him and groused that I had put his back up with my crude talk. "You admire that head of hair," I teased them, knowing it was more. He had winning ways with young and old alike.

Then there he was one afternoon, with presents for them both. A puppy for the boy and a nice painted flowerpot with lilies for the old lady.

"You didn't bring me nothing," I grumbled.

"A faithful student," he said. "When I left here the last time, I had in mind that you were putting me on. The longer I thought of what you said, the more sense it made to me. Best advice I ever heard. So I'm back for more."

"No," I said. "You are back because you reckon to use me. Which will do for beginners. Now get comfortable and I will spell out the details.

"Readying for battle, you must study the ground as well as knowing the capacity of your army and their army. It is not enough to eyeball the ground without grasping how it is classified. We classify ground as honestly inviting or treacherously inviting, which will bog you down. It may also be precipitous or smooth, distant, semidistant, or close. Also you will classify it as ultimate, penultimate, or indecisive. It will be constricting, open, or flanked on one side with hills. Ground which we and the enemy both find inviting is seldom ultimate. On such ground, the advantage might go to him who first takes any high place convenient to his supply routes . . ."

I went on in such wise until his eyes were glazing, having fun with rattling off so much I have brought down to system. Before he fell dead asleep, I called the old lady to bring us some pomegranate juice. Refreshed by it and intuiting the time was ripe, he felt me out some more.

"My father . . . have you given him all this lore you are sharing with me?"

"He didn't have to be told," I said. I laid that out as emphatic as I could, because truly if he went wrong in what he would undertake, I did not want it to be by unworthy blunder. He had great stuff in him, Absalom, and if he lost, I wanted it to be after he had given it his best shot. "You have heard how your father threw down Goliath?"

"I heard something about that, yes."

"How he had no arms, only the five smooth stones he took from a stream?"

Absalom waited for the twist I would give to such detail.

"Why *five?*" I shot at him rapid fire.

He did not attempt to wise off. He let me tell him.

"Why five? No more, no less? Because five is neither too many nor too few. If you can't drop the big fellow with five, you blew it. On the other hand it is prudent to allow for some misses."

"Either four or six would have been a mistake," Absalom said. He was marveling at how exact military science has to be. "And he knew when he picked them up five was right."

"You bet your sweet ass he did. Never a doubt in his mind. Now go mull that over. Put it on top of your meditations. King David did not have to be told what I am telling you."

◈

Yet, knowing he meant mischief against King, I let him keep coming to me on the pretext that what I had learned in my scars and broken bones could be handed along by gab.

It's not one of my poorest memories, those afternoons I spent with Absalom in the back yard rehearsing the art of war.

The fig tree was ripe then. We would put our feet up, chew a fig, and spit the skins onto the gravel while we discussed. My old woman and daughter-in-law would keep an eye on us from the house to see if we needed anything. My grandson would squat in the gravel, all big eyes and ears, to wait for the parts of the story he liked most: castrating captives or the hard marches in the desert. Nice little fellow, though he lacked the physique ever to amount to much as a fighter.

The bees humming. The sound of a churn on our porch. A lazy mule sauntering on the cobblestones. The neighbor chopping weeds out of his vineyard or laying up stone for an addition to his house. I have nothing against peace as such, and there were peaceable sounds all about us while we talked and planned war.

In the dirt of the yard I would draw maps of where I had been and where the Syrian cavalry. "You want in such cases to be like one of them two-headed snakes," I would tell him. "If the Syrian comes at your head head, you bite him with your tail head. Or vice versa. If he hits you in the middle, you bite him with both heads."

"I see." And he did see. With his constitution and brains, he might have made a first-rate general. He could think Syrian and Hebrew at the same time, which is requisite both in planning and execution.

◈

Noting the help I gave him, you will say I led the sheep to water. Yes. But it was Achitophel who made him drink. Myself, I would not ever have openly sided with rebellion as long as King was alive. Sometimes, when I knew for sure the time was nearing, I regarded it almost as a match, where I might lay a small wager on the outcome without other concern.

I admit all of us had reason to be fed up with King in that period. He had not quite come to the melancholy and suspicion that had made Saul such a trial for one and all in his later years. But he had king's blues for sure. Which come from having to answer to the Lord for all the wear and tear a kingdom can give.

He let us go on wallowing in the muck of a bad peace. Wherever you looked was stagnation. The termites in the wood you hear eating your house away when you wake up before morning light, lying comfortably enough with your woman beside you. And wish you were out on the cold stones with a sword alongside and something meaningful to be done.

At such hours, you get to worrying more about the goyim than is reasonable. They are inventing a weapon that will put them ahead. A two-pointed spear that will come up your asshole while puncturing your sternum. A chariot with a team of horses rigged behind so it can go in reverse as fast as forward. Trick wombs on their women so every kid they drop is a Goliath, or has twelve fingers and toes of extraordinary strength for gouging.

Or more sensible concerns about the discipline of the young generation. I don't care whether young folks respect their elders. That is not the main thing. But they ought to respect reality, how tough life really is, or the Philistines might as well take over.

Days Absalom would miss coming by, my tad grandson would circle the yard near to the wall and hedge and from time to time peep into the street when he heard wheels go by.

He said he wished Absalom was his big brother.

Another time, he said he wished Absalom was his father. To which I replied with some force, since his actual father was killed in battle honorably and the boy was wrong to gainsay his pride in that. Well, he wouldn't. He was brought up in my household with proper respect for values. He only meant, he said, "Prince Absalom hugs me a lot when he is here."

"I noticed," I said. "That is because you are such a fine young boy."

"No. It is because he is lonesome."

The lad could not have said that had he observed Absalom working the crowd out in front of the palace or with the young men in the sports arena. But it was what he had seen here, and it was beyond any argument. Everyone sees from his own vantage. There may be truth every grownup will miss.

Another time the kid said outright, "I can't wait for Prince Absalom to be king."

"That's not smart," I chided. "You're already sorry because you think him lonesome. Someday you will know a king has got to be lonesomest of all."

"If he's so lonesome now," he said slowly, "then he has most right to be king."

I couldn't help meditating on that. No conclusion.

◈

I figured a time would have to come when Absalom out and out offered me command of the troops when the rebellion broke. Then I would be in a position where I would have to cut him down then and there or go along.

The whole truth is I had become unsure which way I would go, and he never asked me, though he edged up to it again and again. Often the edge got very thin. "I wonder if my father knows how much he owes you?" he asked one day. A natural prelude to saying he would reward me more according to my deserts.

Another time he put it, "Achitophel says the goyim fear you more than the king."

"I supposed you had been taking counsel with Achitophel."

"He's taught me a lot about foreign policy."

"Should you ever be king, you would need help with foreign policy as well as the army," I said. "Achitophel has traveled widely. There is a lot in his policy that is foreign, all right. But I must tell you there is fear and there is respect. A general is supposed to be like a butcher's dog. Everyone fears him. Should you ever become king, you will need respect as well as fear. I don't know who respects Achitophel that much."

He snorted and said, "I know he has a reputation for being . . . *overelegant* in manners. He doesn't have the common touch."

"He is a fruiter," I said. And there went Absalom's hope he could have both me and Achitophel on his side when the showdown came. But he did not intend I should get any sign of how he had been thinking. He came right back with the defense that in both foreign policy and war the king had to be the final authority.

I pushed on. "You say so now. In the abstract. But as things go, you've sometimes got to count on others in life-and-death matters. I can only speak to the military side and discuss the nature of command. But everyone knows a good army will not see you through if the Lord is not with you. You had better spend some time with Nathan, too, who can tell you how to butter up the Lord."

My sentiment toward Nathan was easier for him to swallow than my disparaging Achitophel. He said, "If I were king, Nathan could cuddle with the other eunuchs. It's listening to Nathan that made my father lose touch with the people. I've seen that clearly."

"It's handy to be sensitive to the people," I said, and he heard no mockery yet in my voice. "That is close to what I will say to you now. A general learns to think of his men as infants. Not comrades. Never pals. He treats them as you see me treat my grandson. So they will march with him in the deep, dry valleys with ambush on every side. In the heat of summer, he doesn't go to the shade of the trees or wrap up in winter. He sees that the men have food before he eats. He dismounts and walks should there be a retreat. Makes sure that all are entrenched before he takes to shelter."

"You spoil them?"

"I'm glad you used the word before I did. Spoiling them is the risk that any leader of men will run — your father included. The troops must be treated as children without letting them become headstrong and useless. The edge between is very fine. Fear has got to balance with perfect love. Do you see my haircut?"

He had not flinched when I called Achitophel the dirty name, but my abrupt question about hair shook him, as it was meant to do. Being sensitive to people's feelings, he had generally kept his eyes off my pate, which was in ugly contrast to his much-admired curls.

I said, "Take a good look now, and I will tell you why I keep it so. Once upon a time, I was almost as bushy-headed as you. Then there was an occasion in a captured town when I had given strict orders there was to be no foraging of victuals. Well, you have seen how I am partial to a nice juicy fig if it is good and ripe, and so in midafternoon while I am hearing a court martial, I find myself absent-mindedly chewing a fig I had reached down from the branch overhead. I saw my captains looking at me kind of funny while I munched. Soon as I gathered my wits, I yelled, 'No excuses, no exceptions. Heads-

man, cut off my head.' The whole army was in an instant up-
roar, and you could not have told from the sound of them
whether I had scared them shitless by going crazy or they was
objecting out of pity for me. Well, after I had let it sink in, I
said, all right, since I was still useful I would keep my head,
but I had my hair chopped off once and for all as a sign.

"That episode was *known* in the army before we all started
to get soft. The story went through the ranks. It was known that
when Joab was in command, orders would be enforced down
to the letter, silly as they might seem."

"Yes," Absalom said. "I always listen hard to what you have
to say. But times have changed."

When I know I am right, I never argue. I simply yelled,
"Why don't you get your hair cut before you tangle with some-
body bigger'n you, Absalom?" Like he was some recruit from
the hill country and not a prince on the verge of being more
than that.

Talk about what works on the nervous system of men, women,
infants, cats, and dogs alike. Threaten their hair unexpectedly
and watch them react. It is out of the primeval past, for sure.

It was the first and only time I saw Absalom show hatred
and fear of me. But flustered as he was, he made a cool exit.
Stayed for another fig and a joke about every man to his own
style, then he walked very leisurely until he was out the gate
and past the corner of the wall.

He gave his horses a dreadful whack, as his chariot went
racing off down the road. To Achitophel's palace in Hebron,
naturally.

My grandson came out to me and crawled into my lap.
"Grandpa, why was Prince Absalom in such a big hurry to
leave?"

"I think I just goosed him in his timetable," I said.

Solomon and Bathsheba

◆

"WHY CAN'T Father be king anymore? Did the Lord measure him and find him wanting?"

"No," Bathsheba said. "It's because he wouldn't listen to me."

David

———◆———

ON ONE OTHERWISE unremarkable day it will just be clear
to you . . . You will bite down on a grain of sand while chewing and find a loose molar. Stoop to pick a flower and jerk the
whole plant out by the roots. A shoestring or harpstring will
snap in routine handling. You will sit back then with the broken
string dangling from your fingers, very pensive as you mull over
the signal.

Take a long, hard look in the mirror if you sincerely want to
know how God sees you today. There are fewer mysteries about
His appraisal than your busy vanities and routine confidence tell
you there are. It is only fogged vision that disguises mortality
for a single ticking second of a lifetime.

In every eye and all the palace mirrors, David saw that he
was grizzled now. He who had puzzled with so many of the
Lord's conundrums understood right well that a *grizzled* David
was a contradiction in terms. An oxymoron to the general.

Once and for all, David is *youth:* the smooth forehead fringed with curls, the well-tempered biceps, the fluent hip, and a belly with shallow dimples.

A heart — the most telling distinction of all between the true David and this absurd caricature — a heart that leaped with the roebucks and sang with nightingales. The heart of the Fool in the Tarot pack.

Now his heart leaped with the old, foolish joy only when . . . he watched Absalom bud and prepare to blossom out as king. The king whom David, at his best, had hoped to be was down in front of the palace in the crowd of ordinary citizens, charming everyone with spendthrift promises. Or he was off in the fields with his contemporaries, tossing spears at lion-skin targets. Enjoying the pure thrill of speed as his red-bronze hair streamed behind his flying chariot.

Royal David was youth and youth was Absalom. It is easier to dispute with the Lord and His prophets than to argue the equations of time that an honest, contrite eye will read.

Nathan whinnied at him, "There was a certain man who had a wayward lamb in his flock. Lo, the man did put that lamb in the charge of a sly fox . . ."

"Achitophel?" Cute as a shithouse rat was the way David privately labeled Achitophel, but he accepted the prophet's metaphor of the fox for the sake of the parable. "You're trying to tell me, Nathan, that pretty soon the lamb's teeth got sharp and his fleece began to look like the fox's fur, and . . ." There was fun but no gain in trying to mock a prophet as single-minded as this one. "Well, what shall we do about it, Nathan? Slaughter the lamb, or the fox, or both of them?"

Nathan bridled at this talk of violence. Was it ever the wise course? He knew of no evidence that capital punishment deterred crime.

"Joab would argue that it deterred Abner very effectively. I see there may be no use in capital punishment after the crime is done. But if you apply it beforehand, hey? You have to admit an axe to the neck slows a criminal down at least."

The mere mention of Joab gave Nathan convulsions. The spittle flew as he denounced "that filthy man" who deserved as much blame as Achitophel for misleading impressionable Absalom. However, *knowing* Absalom to be impulsive and impressionable, could hindsight say it had been wise to bring the youth home from Geshur at all? Perhaps a longer journey in foreign parts would cool down any imprudent ambitions. There was no such thing as a bad boy, of course. What a pity, Nathan ranted on, Absalom had not found more suitable mentors than Achitophel and Joab.

"Like Solomon's?"

"Such a prince, though still so young. Never loud or uncouth. Thoughtful for his elders. No indelicacies. Good grooming. Calmness. There is a prince who honors his father and mother."

No doubt at all that Solomon honored his mother. While Nathan — and so many others — were warning of Absalom's ambitions, David heard the threat from Solomon's partisans without much straining.

He foresaw that they would be able to pull it off, too. If not in the immediate future, then when his beard had gone completely gray. Mother, son, and mentor would whipsaw him beyond his capacity to resist.

In the worst scenario, he saw the mother sometime threatening to publish *Intimate Palace Secrets*. ("He dressed me in sheepskins, even on the hottest nights.") This would make news, and not only among the Hittites, who were still grumbling about Uriah and demanding investigations. They would publish it in Gath, tell it in the streets of Askelon. ("He urged me to bleat like a ewe!!!") No matter if it could be labeled a forgery, it would go a long way among the Philistines unless he paid at the source to suppress it.

If Absalom didn't topple him with a clean sword cut, someday he might find his wine laced with rat poison. On top of all other considerations, he had some preference for going out in soldierly style.

◈

Certainly he could not claim, ever, that he had not been fully warned. Even his harp sang laments about the overthrow of an aging king who had squandered the love of his subjects. In his dreams, cherubim patronized him with divine condescension, alluding to him as "the former king."

Nor could he claim simple indecision. Oh, a time or two he had dallied with the notion of calling Joab back from retirement — or whatever the old devil's status might be — and purging the army. But the truth was he had no stomach for the remedies Joab would propose. Besides this, he had no assurance of which way Joab would jump when push came to shove. Not a nice prospect to face Joab with his hands up his sleeves if he had cut a deal with Absalom.

On balance, it must be admitted that King David had decided to take a dive. Seeing the punch telegraphed, he was halfway to the canvas before it had a chance to connect.

So there he was one night on the palace roof complacently listening to the buzz from the local garrisons as the troops mustered, watching the distant lines of torches as they moved out the gates on the road to Hebron.

Out of the dark behind him came an anonymous whisper, "Milord king, Amasa gave the orders. Only the palace guards will remain."

"Oh, that's good. That's considerate." At least the engineers of the plot did not intend to leave him defenseless should the hoodlum element be tempted to loot the palace and distress the women.

"Amasa, hey?" If Amasa was giving orders, that meant Joab was not with the plotters, for he would hardly accept to be second in command. For a moment of excited possibility, David visualized a way out. What a spectacle could still be staged! Sending Joab along with the deserting troops to Hebron, the ugly bastard springing out like a cunt from a cake at a bachelor party just as General Amasa was congratulating the troops and taking their pledges. Joab kisses Amasa on the cheek and puts the steel in Amasa's back as he did with Abner. What a surprise party for the victors, while Joab leads the cheering. Long live King David!

"Send for Joab and bring him to me," he ordered over his shoulder. No response. Whoever had come in the darkness to warn him had vanished.

Now the torches of the marching columns had disappeared beyond the hills. The stars overhead had moved. The former king began to worry about getting his womenfolk evacuated while the troops were gone and the city gates still unguarded.

For the next hours, he was bogged down in the trivia of hustling wives, eunuchs, baggage, and a little snack for travel down the back stairs.

Bathsheba wasted more of his time than the rest put together. Oh, she was willing to leave with him if milord the king had been such an idiot as to let it come to this. What choice did she have after all the years she sacrificed to his every whim, grown old and put on weight so it was very late in the day to start over again with a new regime? She would not say she would have been better off with Uriah. Had she ever once thrown that up to him? She might not have shoes fit for walking off the pavement on a dark night. But she would keep up with the rest of his crew.

The sticking point was — again — Solomon. She wanted him evacuated on a litter.

"He's a grown boy. He can ride a mule. He can ride *my* mule. I can walk if he can't."

"All week he's been feverish. From worrying about *you*," Solomon's mother said. "You didn't even notice that. A temperature that would cook an egg, and his father wants him to get on his feet and walk out in the night air. How far are we going? Have you arranged where we'll stop and if there will be a doctor there or even decent bedding? How far does milord think we will get tonight?"

"I don't know."

"Hah! See? All right, I'll have poor Solomon at the back door by the time you've taken care of every little whim of your concubines. I suppose *they're* riding in litters, yes. Taking their oil and their perfume and a donkey load of tambourines! We'll be ready, milord."

"I'm leaving the concubines here to take care of things."

"Then it's not as dangerous as you make out. This is just one of your fine entertainments, all arranged."

"Not dangerous for them."

"You mean . . . If Solomon doesn't go, they will kill him? That's what you're unwilling to tell me, isn't it? Or you'll kill him by marching him out on a cold night."

"I don't think they would kill him." Already David was seeing himself in Absalom's place. Absalom in his place. Well, whichever way it went, it came out the same. He would not *bother* killing Solomon once he got going with the heady business of cleaning up the state. Just give the lad a doll's house with some toy concubines and later a nifty allowance to buy up some art —

that would be a statesmanlike solution to the Solomon problem. Solomon, rightly handled, could be an ornament to bring tourism into the city.

King David said nothing of the sort in the face of Bathsheba's outrage, for, *lo*, the bitterness that had been griping him for such a long while was peeling away. By God, he didn't know where, or even whether, his little band of fugitives would sleep tonight, tomorrow, or the next night.

By God, it was a good feeling to be hitting the road again, likely sleeping under bushes and drinking rainwater when they were lucky enough to get it. Too much good wine had left a sour taste in his mouth. All he thirsted for was to be away from this hassle.

"Look," he said kindly to Bathsheba. "I'll tell you where you and Solomon — and take Nathan, of course — can hide out in the city until you can cut a deal with Absalom."

"A place where you've sneaked out for your lewd parties! Where you've kept the fancy women you wouldn't let come here!"

"Well, take it or leave it," David said. There was a spring in his step as he skipped into the night.

Passing out through the dark gate of the city, sure at last that Bathsheba and her son were not coming with him on his flight, he felt his lungs expand with relief and something close to glee. Certainly, he hoped the exasperating woman would be safe in whatever haven she chose within the walls, but he worried about her less and less with every delicious step he took away from her.

Joab

———◆———

SOMETIMES I GUESS wrong. It was honed down so fine I
had thought that at the last a messenger would come either
from King or from Absalom asking me to take charge of the
military.

When I knew the balloon was up and Absalom had chosen
Amasa to get the troops to Hebron where him and Achitophel
was centering their scheme, then I thought King would call me
to rally the troops still loyal. I probably would have done it if
asked and could have forced a draw at least.

King let it go by default. He disappointed me there. Even
when he is cunt-struck and playing too much harp, he is at core
a fighter.

But there it was, and now I must think out my strategy with
the new crowd. It seemed to me I could find my berth to do my
trade with the new as with the old. Though he had appointed
Amasa first, Absalom would not forget what I told him about
the butcher's dog, and Achitophel would underline they needed
one. Knowing how I am feared abroad.

I will state this, however, as it bore on the outcome. I was sick disgusted with the way Absalom's pansy adviser had him show the people of Jerusalem who was now boss.

King had left ten of his concubines behind in the palace when he headed for the boonies. They were left to red up the house and pack away family mementos in case he could ever claim them.

So Achitophel has a tent set up on the palace roof. In which he places couches and the ten concubines. With all Jerusalem gathered down below to watch, that bushy-headed Absalom goes in unto his father's women.

Not that there was any lewdness to the spectacle. The action was all inside the tent. But the silly crowd began to count at the top of their voices. "One. Two. Three. Four. Five! Six! Seven! Eight! NINE!!" And then a mighty roar. "TEN!!!!" And Absalom, following his earlier reputation, was the new sex champion, as well as king.

You can see how low the people have got when the pecker counts more than the sword.

David Himself

◆

FAIR SKY in the morning and no sign of pursuit on the road from Jerusalem. The adventure is unrolling just as he might have dreamed.

His mule is frisky with the morning's fresh delight. He rides it back and forth up the column of wives, children, and faithful retainers who have come out with him. The whole palace staff — minus cooks — seems to have chosen to go along.

There is a larger band in the march than you might guess. In recent years, the wife count has not been very exact. A surprising number of the children look like him. He halts the mule to make friends with a curly-head of under ten, who wants to know, "Why didn't we ever do this before, Father?"

"I'm glad you think it's fun. But when we get up in the hills, the bears will come out at night."

Without a word, the boy holds out for inspection . . . a *sling*. He rattles a pocketful of pebbles. So much for bears.

"Good!" his father commends.

"Can you show me how to use it?"

"Well, son, I'm a little rusty. Here, I'll give it a try. Hey, these are nice smooth pebbles you've found. Very best kind."

He winds up and slings at a raven crossing the column diagonally on its ominous business. Knocks the bird out of the air with the first stone cast.

"Wizard!" says the wide-eyed boy. "Do that again."

Deflection shooting is nothing to trifle with, even when the Living God guides your arm. "Another time." David laughs. He tosses the sling back into the boy's hands and turns the mule away. "Get some practice as we go, and don't forget the bears. I see some good folks I want to parley with."

Not all those who have taken to the road with him are blood kin or paid retainers. There are men and women of Jerusalem who must continue to love him for his own sake, since they have reason to suppose they would fare better at home with Absalom than with him in the desert. A rainbow collection of the elderly, the infirm, sojourners, and dispossessed, but also a stream of able-bodied chaps who have come along fully armed. Enough of them to sting if the new monarch tries to round them up.

One of these is Joab's brother Abishai — not exactly Joab's equal in either craft or ferocity but no slouch in close combat. It must be said of him as well that he has a more candid face than Joab's and a simple heart to match his countenance. From their exchange of greetings, David believes he recognizes the voice that, last night, delivered a loyal warning to him.

Among the armed men is a company-strength band of Gittites (mere immigrants from last year's famine in the South) hupping along in a disciplined formation while a man named Itai counts cadence. Swept by the generous mood of the morning, David gallops alongside, slows his mule, and rather fulsomely expresses welcome and gratitude. His exuberant phrases get no response from Itai. David guesses the fellow may not yet have a command of Hebrew. Perhaps the language barrier has betrayed him into a pitiable mistake. He and his men may not even know that during the night a revolution has taken place.

"Me no more king," David says in pidgin Hebrew. "This not line of duty. Face about. Go back to barracks. Explain not get orders straight. Patch up. Absalom king now. Absalom much good fellow, ho, ho. Not be cruel. Explain to Amasa. Him also good fellow. Stay away from Joab. Joab chop, chop head. *Capisco?*"

Now Itai turns a face livid with outrage. Foreigner he may be, but he will not be mocked when he is trying his best. "I spik Hebrew good as you, yis?" he froths. "Yis, I spik Hebrew good. Where King go, Itai go. In life, in death. King's servant will be with, yis."

How's that for good Hebrew? David gallops to the head of his column again, his eyes glowing with the unpredictable fun of it all.

Memories old as the flight from Egypt quicken in him and his gorgeous rabble. In the first bright hours of escape, all share the revivalist spirit that burns in his bosom hot enough to singe his cloak. If he took them to the Red Sea, by God, who could doubt the water would part to let them pass now that they have shucked off the oppression of the city?

And, yes, there in the high morning, above the gleaming mountaintops, God has set a cloud of celestial white to lead them to the land perpetually promised.

◈

Women came out of the groves along the road carrying bundles of oranges and figs and skins of goat milk for them. Children with sun-darkened skin and sun-bleached hair trailed alongside the procession until they were scared to be so far from home and fell back. In the fields, groups of distant farmers paused in their work. Time after time, as the refugees passed such groups, David heard their voices raised in what he took to be cheering.

He said to his old wife Akinoam, "It's refreshing to be back with simple folks. Just think, they may not get the news out here for many days yet."

"They are wailing," Akinoam said.

"Oh."

"For the king who failed them."

Just as she spoke, he saw that the guiding cloud was rapidly darkening, like a blotter soaking up ink.

◈

Still, a cloud is a cloud, and when you have nothing better to direct you, you have to keep following it. Presently, it led them across the brook Kidron. Here the cultivated fields, roads, and vineyards were left behind. There were, indeed, paths on the far side, but they were the melancholy little tracks of nomads and the itinerant poor who endured their brutish lives in the wilderness.

At a crossing in the foothills, where the tracks came together like slack strands of a web, waiting for the king as if they had positioned themselves before the rebellion, were the priest Zadok and all his murmuring Levites with him.

Unimpressed with worldly politics, they had brought the Ark of the Covenant to be with the anointed king even if he ran like a rabbit.

Carried out by litter, the Ark sat now on an altar-shaped stone, humming and buzzing with power. Swarming insects would not come near it. A bird looking for a perch was incinerated in midair as it prepared to land on the holy box, turned into a puff of smoke that stank of burnt feathers.

"Take it back to Jerusalem, Zadok," David ordered. "I appreciate the gesture, but it wouldn't work. I have promises to keep and miles to go before I sleep." He pointed to the black cloud that was now hovering over the entrance to a mountain pass, beckoning him forward. Lightning came out of the cloud and then a sheet of rain to hide what lay beyond. David said, "If I shall find favor in the eyes of the Lord, He will bring me back and show me both the Ark and His habitation. But if He never again finds delight in me, let Him do with me and mine as He sees fit."

For a minute, the humming in the Ark was the only sound. Then it went dead silent, the juice turned off. Zadok motioned for his Levites to shoulder it again for the trek home.

"Wait!" David said. "I may have spoken hastily. What I should have said was that it will take a little time to sort this tangle out. Absalom may find that it's not all a bed of roses. If I find my grass roots support is still out here, maybe in a week or a month I'll give you a better answer. In the meantime you and your sons — that's Ahimaaz and Jonathan, am I right? — can keep your eyes open around Jerusalem to see if Absalom takes hold. If he doesn't, why you could bring the Ark out again and we can start from there."

Zadok had ceased to listen. The Ark rode in dreadful silence on the shoulders of its bearers.

◈

The black, drenching, gusting cloud no longer guided them. They were climbing right into the thick of it, and as the down-pour grew more savage, the stones underfoot became sharper and more precipitous. In the density of falling water, the air seemed thinner and hard to breathe. They slipped in mud and the handhold bushes tore away from the saturated earth.

All around him, strong men were weeping like the women

and children, each for himself and none for the banished king. In no way was he leading them into the reviving hardship of exile. They were leaderless in God's storm. David barely had the authority of husband or father over the least of them.

Now he knew the ghastly difference between leading and bringing. He had brought them into the badlands, old sport, imagining vainly he could retro-fit the past and pull the Moses gambit.

You can't repeat the past. The god he had delivered his people to was not the old time Lord of Israel's hosts, but the very modern god of pure, blind chance. The dice-roller. The gambler who did not even need to load his dice, since human folly had fixed the odds in his favor.

Beside him now, like a little ghost in the ghostly streamers of cold rain, was the unfamiliar son who had brought out his sling only hours ago, down on the flatland. The boy was whimpering now. "How much farther? I'm cold. I'm hungry. I want to go home."

"We'll get to the top soon now."

"You shouldn't have killed that bird."

"I suppose not."

And when they all straggled at last to the crest of the stone ridge, they saw some breaks in the cloud ahead, though it only parted to reveal a tangle of slopes, dun as an ash heap. David ordered that an altar should be set up. He led the people in a thanksgiving service.

"What are we giving thanks for?" Akinoam asked.

"That we survived this far."

Still the song of thanksgiving had a hearty ring to it. Suppress everything but the sound of worship and any of them could imagine being back safe in the tabernacle of the city. And maybe it was only David, the best king they had left, who knew they were worshiping the way the dice had fallen this time.

◈

The Lord was mum. It was men and beasts who brought them comfort on the far side of the mountain. Some way down from the dank crest, there came Ziba, the servant, with a couple of donkeys loaded with provisions. Bread, raisins, fruit, and wine. The little animals stopped to be unloaded, twitching their long ears and smiling cute little donkey smiles at the gratitude they produced with their timely arrival. Belly is god, they seemed to be saying, and we are rightly known to be servants of god.

David gobbled with the rest. After his ordeal, there was no reason he shouldn't. His kingship, with its bracing responsibilities, had been pretty thoroughly washed away in the rain.

He had his eye on the donkeys, since his mule had bolted long before they came to the top of the ridge. It seemed right to claim a ride down from here. Perks of age and masculinity, if not of kingship anymore. He would let Akinoam ride the smaller animal.

As the victuals sharpened his wits, David grew curious how a bond servant like Ziba should be out here on his own. Ziba served Mephibosheth, one of Saul's descendants to whom David had been particularly kind in better days.

"Where's your master, Ziba?"

"Back in Jerusalem. Big day for him. Celebrating the new king. Lots of bonfires."

Mmmmm. So much for kindness. The ingratitude was hard to take for a man on the verge of a lousy cold from exposure.

Ziba expanded. "Master thinks he may be the new king pretty soon."

"As a matter of fact, the new king is my son Absalom."

"Not for long, master says. Master says, with David on the run, it's up for grabs."

"I see."

"Master says House of Saul can't screw it up worse."

"He's got a point. If that's what he's got in mind, just what are you doing out here? A spy?"

Ziba shrugged without bothering to deny it. "Doesn't look like you got much left worth spying on. I brought you raisins, didn't I?"

Put a gift raisin in your mouth and keep it closed, David.

Contritely, the former king yielded both donkeys to the women. He should be grateful they didn't ride him piggyback.

◈

Shimei, another buzzing insect from the House of Saul, got to him next, before they were even down to the valley floor. Out of a hovel the eye could hardly distinguish from debris left by the storm hobbled the very dirty and tattered old man.

"You bloody man, you! You *David*, you!" Shimei yelled, waving both fists. "Jew bastard! Whorehopper! Maggot in a piece of camel shit!"

He paused to catch another breath and to throw a rock across the gully. It rang on the shield that Abishai raised to protect the draggled king.

Shimei raged on. "Thought when you got rid of Saul, the Lord would let you fart through silk the rest of your days. You thought so. Well, look at you now. Big bloody turd."

"Let me go get him," Abishai growled. The cursing had upset all of David's remnant. Though reverence was already a fading habit, this struck them as blasphemy.

"Stay where you are," David ordered. Abishai let his blade go back in the sheath.

"Sheep-fucker!" Shimei bellowed and threw another stone. Abishai deflected again.

David began to laugh mightily. This was what Goliath had called him once, so very long ago. The last syllables the giant got out before young David climbed all over him.

He still didn't hanker to be called a sheep-fucker to his face. But for just a minute he'd heard in Shimei's blathering the voice of God again, addressed to him. Which was somewhat better than dead silence from on high.

"We will cross Jordan this evening," King David said. His voice of command came out firmly, in the old way.

Solomon

◆

My mother has doves' eyes.

I wrote that out for Bathsheba on vellum with my calligraphic pen. I scented the page with myrrh and spikenard and left it where I knew she would find it.

"Oh, you little poet, you," she said. She hopes I will write much more in the same style.

Absalom

———◆———

SURE ENOUGH, there came Nathan with his forefinger raised
and his voice droning its falsetto of rebuke: "Lo, there was a
certain *man* who had ten sheep. And when this *man* was summoned away by night, he did leave these sheep in charge of his
son, that *they* might safely graze. And lo . . . !"

Yep. The treacherous son did whip out his tool and most
lewdly damage all those ewes. In public view.

"Who hath done this dreadful thing?" King Absalom demanded. "As the Lord liveth, if he coupled with *ten* sheep, he
must surely die ten times over."

"*Thou art the man!*" Nathan said, bringing his line off with
full dramatic value. He went up on the balls of his feet to wait
for it to sink in, as once it had sunk into the whippersnapper's
father.

No rise. Was Absalom as stupid as he was lascivious?

"Those ten sheep were thy father's concubines thou didst de-
file. In public view. I myself saw small boys counting and cheering below the palace wall."

"Six!" cried Absalom, holding up crossed fingers in Nathan's puckered face. "As the Lord liveth, I only got to six of them."

Who'd have thought the old man could suck in so much air? If he had been impassioned when he came here, this trifling impudence drove his fury past bounds. If there was ever an excuse for capital punishment, the Lord beheld it now. One howitzer blast of lightning, O Lord send down!

No lightning came from heaven. No viper crawled up the leg of the throne to bite the usurper. Wheezing lungs can only hold the breath of indignation for so long. Then the Lord's business comes down to bargaining, man to man.

"I admit it was ill-advised," Absalom said. The word was, in fact, entirely apt. Left to his own inclinations, he would not have touched those concubines his father had left behind when he fled. Achitophel was the rascal who had concocted the foolish spectacle, with his usual complexity of reasoning. Achitophel had urged the need for a symbolic gesture. Something which, once and for all, would be a sign to the people that there was an irreparable breach between father and son, the old king and the new. "An abomination!" Achitophel said. "You can't beat a downright abomination if you want your message heeded and remembered. Something the rabble will regard as beyond your father's forgiveness."

In hindsight, Achitophel's advice was terrible. It led, first, to Absalom's fudging on the count. From the street he heard the crowd shouting "TEN!" when they supposed he had shagged all the women in the tent on the palace roof. Which was smelling pretty gamy by that time.

The real score was more like seven. Or six and three-quarters. Actually six and a third, when it came down to the bitter truth. He was not more than two and a half inches into the seventh (name of Belisa? the fancy one from Galilee was all he could remember as identification) when his wilt had to be accepted as final. The last three had not even stripped. He would not soon forget their contemptuous glares.

Achitophel had laughed deliriously when he learned of the discrepancy. "Royal concubines are not like those pigs in Geshur, hey, my boy? More *give* and more *take,* would you say?"

"I thought I could make ten. At three and four I had got a second wind and steadied the pace."

"Never mind the body count. Don't give it a second *thought.* The important thing is the symbolism. Perfect!"

Nonetheless, the episode had flushed a whole new covey of anxieties into the open. So much for symbolism.

It brought on the need for continued fudging after his joke with Nathan had — inevitably — misfired. To the prophet, he could not even blame it on Achitophel. Nathan might not approve of Achitophel's sybaritic lifestyle; still, he deplored prejudice directed at anyone whose sexual preference deviated from the norm. There was no *normal* sex as far as Nathan was concerned. Perhaps that was why sheep parables came to him so readily.

So the fidgeting new king was dragged down to lame excuses: "All in the flush of victory, you understand. Emotion running high when we came in from Hebron. The ladies themselves had evidently been into the palace wine. They may have suggested the party. At any rate, the tent flaps were down. Children under twelve couldn't have seen what went on inside . . . Circumstances alter cases, as you would be the first to admit."

"Not . . . wise . . . at . . . all!"

"I agree completely. You know I mean to set a nice moral tone now that things are leveling off. Simple, everyday food. Wine maybe twice a year for the holidays. I'll think about bringing my wife in from Geshur. Maybe no concubines at all. Certainly not *ten.* Everyone will see there's a strict distinction between housekeepers and chambermaids and such concubines as I might — in time — see fit to add."

This line seemed well chosen for Nathan. But he still warned: "A king is only as good as the counsel he receives. He must know the Lord's requirements."

"You'll always have access, Nathan. Every day after breakfast, if that suits your schedule. I hear you get up early."

Better yet. But not quite enough, if the twinkle in the prophetic eye was to be trusted. "To set the moral tone you so wisely proclaim, O King, to silence the distressing rumors, to give a signal quickly to parents wondering what to tell their youngsters about that *tent,* may I firmly recommend that you bring the Queen Mother to the palace before you bring your wife from that other country?"

"The . . . 'Queen Mother'?" *That* was a stopper. In all his days, Absalom had never heard the term used.

"The virtuous Bathsheba."

"That certainly merits thinking about! I'm not quite sure that father would let her come back. Not after the episode we've been discussing, I mean."

"She is in Jerusalem at this hour, O King."

"She didn't go out with him?" The prospect was more palatable as Absalom reflected that Bathsheba had shrewdly seen where advantage lay.

"O King, if I present your proposal to her this morning, I can virtually promise she and Prince Solomon will eat at your table tonight."

So Solomon came as part of the bargain, did he? A premonition warned Absalom that if the boy and Achitophel saw much of each other, they would find they had a great deal in common. The swish of delicate handkerchiefs would whisper innuendos a straightforward king would have trouble following. In the long run, not good at all.

"Let's not hurry the Queen Mother, Nathan. I'll send word once I've had a chance to weigh the matter. If you'd just tell me how to reach her . . ."

"Through me," Nathan said and closed his lips in what might have been a smile.

◈

"A surgical strike!" Achitophel said. The handkerchief he carried was purple today. It swished through the air like a symbolic scimitar, trailing a perfume not at all like the odor of blood.

"It's not yet clear to me that we have to — or want to — kill my father," Absalom said. "We talked of it, yes. I understand you can't make an omelet without cracking eggs. Right enough! But the revolution went so smoothly, after all."

"A comic operetta!" Achitophel intoned. "A parade, and presto chango, the old king is no more. *Le roi est mort, vive le roi. Vive Absalom.* Symbolism is only a part of realpolitik, my boy, more's the pity perhaps. The symbolism was, I may say, most delicately orchestrated. Indeed, it was handsomely done to have Amasa in command of the troops instead of that fiend Joab. How you could have stood his smell all those afternoons you *sat at his feet,* I can hardly fathom. Yet, much as I loathe him, I must say that we need a Joab now for the surgical strike that has become necessary."

"*Not* necessary! My father deserves, at least, to fade away comfortably in exile."

"Aha! You have your pretty fable. Can you really imagine David — the great David — content to fade away? You perceive him as a father. That is understandable. I will concede he let go more easily than we had a right to expect. But *now!* Word comes to him: Absalom fucked my concubines. Made an abominable public show of it.

"Well, *think,* my boy. He is sitting out there under a palm tree contentedly playing his harp. Thoughts tending toward *amour.* Not even a son could doubt his thoughts have a tropism of that sort famous throughout the land. So in the mood of amorous song, he *remembers:* 'That fox Absalom got into my hen coop.' "

"I see," Absalom said.

"It's not beyond the realm of possibility that he could scrape an alliance with what's left of the House of Saul. Nothing is beyond the realm of possibility, unless we act with requisite, perfectly logical firmness now. Who would eat the kernel must crack the nut."

"You might have spelled this out for me before."

"To be utterly candid, my boy . . ."

"You didn't think I had the guts to see it through to the end."

"I *knew* you to be an idealist. I *knew* you were beloved by the people — as your father had ceased to be. The historic moment was at hand. Let it be said of Achitophel that in serving you I served historic necessity. I make no defense against such a charge." He gave another historical flourish of the purple handkerchief as he rested his case.

"But since we can't send Joab on your surgical strike," Absalom said slowly, "I'll tell Amasa to go after him."

"Yes! And bring him back here for a fair trial! Splendid! We'll call the concubines you defiled for character witnesses! Come now. We have no Joab on our team. Give me twelve thousand men, and I'll take care of our problem before the sun sets tomorrow."

"March with a following wind?"

"That has the right sound to it. Push him, I say. Don't let him recover his balance. Run him and the misfits who went out with him, so all the world will see where the wind is blowing now. Cancel the king, and I promise his followers will all come

"It has crossed my mind that having the Queen Mother here with me might be the proper symbolic gesture to assure the public they can expect continuity," King Absalom said for openers. "Achitophel?"

Achitophel had a saffron handkerchief this day. It disguised the trembling of his hands. Nevertheless his glibness was intact. "No one honors Bathsheba more than I," he began. "A woman whose beauty is matched with *savoir-vivre*. Are we in accord on that? And when a woman has brains to match her beauty, I observe it to be the prudent course to have her where one can keep an eye on her. Twenty-four hours a day."

"Not more than twelve or fourteen hours," the king said with a grating chuckle. See how poisoned the atmosphere had become from the indiscriminate symbolism? Not even by innuendo should it be put out that he was giving the concubine treatment to a woman who might soon, indeed, be cheered in the streets as "Queen Mum."

"How says my respected friend Hushai?" the king asked now.

David's apparatchik said, "Where Bathsheba goes, can Solomon be far behind? Now Solomon is wise. If he is not too wise for his own good — as he might be — he is too wise for the good of a king with other matters requiring his vigilance. Let Bathsheba and her Solomon simmer at the back of the stove. The time may indeed come when she will again adorn the palace. Not yet."

"Hushai has spoken better than Lord Achitophel," Absalom said. And nicked two birds with one stone, you bet. Achitophel was glaring blue murder.

"Now to the more pressing matter," Absalom said. "Reluctantly, I have come to agree with Lord Achitophel that my father must be eliminated. At least captured and . . . what to do with him as captive must also be weighed, I admit. I've tried to put personal feelings aside on this grave matter. The only

back with me, and you can see that they have a chicken in
pot, we can balance the budget, advance on the new fr
hey, my boy?"

"I have listened to you carefully," Absalom said. "For
time. Now I want to ask this, Lord Achitophel."

"Yes?"

"That you stop calling me 'my boy.' Fair enough?"

"Fair enough, O King."

"What your king thinks is that, in spite of your very
qualities, you are not the man to make a surgical strike
King David. As you point out, we must consider him still

"Amasa then?"

"Amasa doesn't make surgical strikes. It's against his re
I will reflect more before I make my decision. You ha
vantages of experience I know I lack. Come back tomorro
we'll talk this over again with the faithful Hushai."

◈

Who was the "faithful Hushai"? Well, the bare, outra
and ironic truth of the matter is that Hushai was a mole,
left behind by tricky King David. Hushai was in Jerusal
this historic moment on the exiled king's explicit orde
scatter disinformation wherever it would make the most m
for the usurpers. The Greeks who left a fine wooden ho
the beach for the Trojans had nothing on our hero David
matter of wiliness. Hushai's first service was to befog the
meeting called by the new king, stalling for time, and post
any effective decision.

Wiggling his toes under the conference table, King Al
opened the meeting of advisers by calling first on Lord
tophel to examine the merits of bringing Bathsheba and So
forthwith to lodge in the palace.

justification for dealing with my father must be the good of the kingdom, present and future."

"Without further delay," said Achitophel with a nasty snap of the saffron handkerchief, making it sound like a rope cracking a neck, although a cloud of scent was scattered in the air.

"Lord Achitophel has recommended the dispatch of twelve thousand men at once. Does Hushai agree this is the way to proceed? If so, let him speak briefly, for the shadows of afternoon are already lengthening."

"It might work," Hushai said. "I suppose you are joking about the number of men who might actually saddle up for the mission. Very likely you should subtract a zero from the figure. You could ask Joab how reliable a muster is likely to be. The captains will tell you thousands when they can't produce a hundred properly armed and victualed . . ."

"The king asked for brevity," Achitophel snapped.

Hushai shook his head mournfully. "I did not suppose he asked for a snap judgment where the cost of error might be so great. Consider, King Absalom, that your father and his loyalists are mighty men of war. Consider the state of mind they must be in at this time. Think of a bear robbed of its whelps. Who would venture to face the creature one-to-one? Or even twenty-to-one? Fifty, of course. You could run over them with such odds and take your father.

"*If*, that is, they came on him in the open with all his men. Most unlikely, I would say. If I know anything of your father, he is hid in some pit or a narrow place among the mountains. Joab must have told you something of the importance of terrain."

"Yes or no?" Achitophel demanded. "Ride? Or let him slip away and build up his forces?"

"There is that side of it as well," Hushai conceded. "In battle, as I have known it, and as you must have heard of it from the experience of Joab himself, nothing is simple."

Enjoying the drift his privilege permitted, Absalom cut in, "As a matter of fact, sir, Joab's maxim is just the other way around. 'In war everything is simple, but the simple becomes very difficult.' I just like to keep things straight."

Hushai nodded approvingly. "You have learned well from Joab. And Joab is matchless in the field. Which makes me wonder whether in this present matter — considering all the dangers of ambush in bad terrain, and others I won't spell out for the sake of brevity — whether Joab isn't the better choice for some eventualities, begging the pardon of Amasa, for whom I also have the greatest respect."

"I'll abide by the king's orders," Amasa growled from his corner, where he had been so quiet. "Let me point out though that since I have been publicly named to lead the host . . ."

"Gentlemen! Please!" Achitophel actually began to rip his handkerchief into little ribbons.

There he stood, with the shreds dangling from his trembling fingers. He stiffened his neck then, and said haughtily, "It is plain that I and my counsel have become a joke. I may have been wrong, I may have been right. We will know by the test of battle, which I now see is to be fought by some other means which — *eventually* — you will agree on. Tomorrow. The day after. Next year. So be it.

"But this I have to say, milord King, I do not deserve to be laughed at."

"Why don't you," said Absalom, "go somewhere and drop dead?"

Which, as Scripture certifies, is exactly what Achitophel did.

Stumbled out, got on his horse, and rode home. Hanged himself then and there. *And was buried in the sepulchre of his father.*

There is a moral here for those who can disentangle it.

David

♦

THERE ARE philosopher kings and real kings. If David had been in the former category, the great range of experience thus far in his life would have brought him to a number of useless conclusions. He was the genuine article. What he retained from the onslaught of experience was a healthy capacity for surprise — amazement at his own impulses as much as at the ways of mankind and nature. So he was moved to wonder at how different everything looked from the East Bank.

Wet and bedraggled from Jordan's waters, he stood to watch the rest of his people come over from his lost kingdom. Women and children and elderly persons riding the shoulders of their mighty sons. The company of Itai looked grim and battle-ready as they shook water like wolfhounds and resumed their tight formation. Waiting on the West Bank for their turn to cross, he saw an incredible number of banners and armed men.

"The children of Ammon," Abishai told him. "They're with us now."

Good heavens. According to all logic, the children of Ammon should be taking advantage of his vulnerability to avenge themselves for past atrocities he had laid on them. No sir. They blamed the atrocities on Joab. With the passage of time they had convinced themselves that if their conqueror had been *the king himself* instead of bloody Joab, the women would not have been raped, nor their infants tossed up and caught on spears. They inferred that now David would set about punishing Israel, and they wanted to be in on it.

Thus his authority began to rebuild from the very tide that had swept it away. It was not to be the same authority he had used up over the years in Jerusalem. In some measures it was less and in some measures more than he was once accustomed to. At first, it was so unlikely that he was afraid to test it.

It came, of course, from the Lord. As all his authority had come. Amen. Wasn't the point chiefly that the Lord showed a different visage here on the East Bank? Even that He *was* different among the corn-fed villagers, tribesmen, and soldiers of fortune than He who resided near the Ark in Zadok's keeping. That was a thought verging on blasphemy for a good monotheist. So be it. Where but at the dreadful edge of blasphemy could the Living God be discovered?

◈

The wives who had crossed over with him let him know he was a better man than he had been when he sat on the Jerusalem throne. The savvy women saw that a new beginning for him was a new beginning for them. There is nothing women crave more than new beginnings of the same old thing. Sweeping the hearth, washing the cookware. Birds to warble the same old songs of spring.

Seeing him uncircumstanced, the wives took advantage and

gave it back in mystic simplicities. They made cakes for him — getting him to stir the batter. He dressed the meat for supper. The good wives smirked as they taught him how to season the gravies. They took their meals together with a merriment great to behold.

"Will you play us a nice little song?" they asked demurely after supper.

It delighted him to do just that. The harp sounded better with an appreciative audience. The wily thing seemed to know — if not actually to arrange — which wife would lie with him on any given night. The woman musically chosen would begin to yawn before the others and leave the circle of lamplight to drift bedward. The others would watch her egress with no tinge of jealousy, as if what was in store for her was their pleasure as well. Which, of course, it was on following occasions. No counting or scorekeeping was even thought of. The harp had so sweetened time and taken away its harshness there was no use measuring it enviously.

Pleasure and procreation fell back into their natural harmonious relationship. Within a span of several weeks, half of the women he heartily embraced were cheerfully pregnant.

Religion, too, profited from the new beginning. Here they had none of Nathan's seminars on sensitivity and social problems. The ecstatic folk banged their tambourines in the open air, danced, and made prayers with no trick clauses. The Ark might be far away and maybe the Lord as well, but the joyful noise they made was enough to attract His attention across any imaginable distance.

❖

And yet the harp-dazzled, unphilosophical king stumbled on new paradoxes. The dearer his other wives became to him from health and good behavior, the more he missed . . . Bathsheba.

Of course she had become a nag. Gone over to being more a
mother to Solomon than wife to him. For a long while she had
missed no occasion to rile him. She made him pay through the
nose for rare gallops in her bed. He was not blind to the dimming of her physical charms. She had put on weight, not much
of it in the right places. No mistaking where Solomon got his
tendency to obesity. The king had even come on graffiti in the
palace latrine that spoke to her "unpleasing plumpness."

Waddle she might, his Bathsheba, in the disguise of age.
There was still something about the thought of her that made
his nose twitch in remembrance when he wakened late at night
so far from home, in the embrace of a kinder wife.

What had really happened between him and that impossible
woman which partook of eternity? Had singled her out from the
other wives who preceded and followed?

God knew — and made David sigh through many nights for
answers He was not ready to share.

◈

Almost as absorbing as the mysteries of a sexual nature (and
perversely intermingled with them) were his reflections on
political authority. Once when he had brought some political
worry to Bathsheba, she had cut him off impatiently, saying,
"Oh, handle those twerps the way you handle me." The only
times he *could* handle her were when she was wound up to
preorgasmic lubricity, requiring his nudge to roll her boulder-
er for her. Nevertheless, her offhand comment had charmed
him.

Taken at face value, it was as much a sanction for his past
career as formula for perpetual success. Right on! He *had* fucked
a number of potential adversaries during the first years of his

rule. Well-fucked, they had mostly died without understanding his hand was in the matter, whoever might have swung the blade.

Take Abner. (That most persistent ghost, who really might have expected David's sympathy for being in trouble over a woman.) There had been insistent *raisons d'état* for dropping this key leader. If Saul's loyalists were going to make a successful confederation, who but Abner could have welded the factions? Therefore . . .

As Joab had said, "Therefore . . ." Pulling his finger across his throat.

What an appalling thought to wake to now in his nights of reflection. Now or then, King David would have no part of it. Neither his face nor his voice had assented to bloody Joab's recommendation. But surely he had fucked Abner by sending Joab to call the man to Jerusalem for further negotiations, knowing full well that Joab had old scores to settle. That little matter of Abner's killing Joab's brother Asahel . . .

Died Abner as a fool dieth? Here in the village of Mahanaim, where Abner had had his turn in exile long ago, David came to no conclusions.

No need pressed him to weep for Abner, *seeing that he was dead.*

However he sent them flying, his thoughts circled back to his own destiny. All he was truly sure of was that it was not yet fulfilled. Bloody and blundering as he had been, was there not still a chance to do better?

◈

To be a great king you must confess freely you have been a bad one.

Yes but no. That was too glib and philosophical altogether

to suit the enormous task still unaccomplished. It reduced the office and the mystic crown to the individual who wore the trappings. It implicated the Lord (Who had bestowed the crown, after all, and Who partook in whatever emanated from it in the march of merely temporal events). It blamed the Lord for transient personal failings. Truly, any king whatever will have frailties and dream bad dreams because he must act in time that is not the Lord's time. Go beyond that to admit there are snares and temptations in the office that are bound to magnify the king's human shortcomings. Shall the Author and Partner in kingship be dragged through the mire of human remorse?

God forbid.

Therefore King David, wintering in Mahanaim, will acknowledge but not repent all malfeasance laid to his charge by his own conscience.

He will hearken to the cursing of Shimei (what a fury of vituperation!) but is not accountable to him.

Here, beyond the Jordan, the harpist tunes his instrument for melodies appropriate to the old age he is advancing to meet. This long spell of absence from the Jerusalem throne is not to be a renewed adventure of youth. The voyage is inward and upward, not back to the potency of his salad days.

What if his singing voice no longer charms birds out of the trees? The harp still speaks for his best self, changing imperfections and crimes into deathless song, filling in gaps of logic when he fails to think philosophically of what he has been and still must be.

Thou preparest a table before me in the presence of mine enemies.

Someone did. The town of Mahanaim boomed that winter. Honey, and butter, and sheep, and cheese of kine poured in from the countryside to feed the burgeoning kingdom in exile.

To join him came mighty men with axes, bows, halberds, javelins, armor, shields, and chariots.

◈

It was a market day in spring when King David took his customary walk through the village — if Mahanaim could still be called a village. Certainly it would not have looked familiar to Abner if that unfortunate man had come back. Through the winter it had swelled to fifty, a hundred, a thousand times its former population. Now it was a humming garrison with suburbs of tents as far as the eye could mark. Merchants and sutlers had followed the soldiers in, as had women of all descriptions, naturally. And where there were women there was a building boom, as well as entertainment by night and day. Call it an eyesore in its unplanned sprawl. Still, it throbbed in the spring sunshine with the vigor of war to come.

In the ankle-deep dust of the market, King David sniffed the fresh lettuces and the tang of early fruit. Most trees had been cut for firewood, but birds twittered in the blue air fresh from the mountains, as they jostled for perches on the poles of the market tents. Soldiers came to attention as the King came up to them nibbling a fresh pomegranate he had filched from a vendor.

This morning it was Itai's turn to take the stroll with his king. "Good day, yis. Good day for fight. Go get'm, yis?"

"We must wait for the trumpet of the Lord."

"Blow loud, yis? Scare shit out of rebels."

"It will be loud enough. We will know it when we hear it."

Itai made a sound of agreement, though it was apparent he wakened every morning to the sound of the divine bugle.

"Who is that mighty man down by the wall?" the king asked, squinting into the sun.

"Keep coming all the time. Plenty soldiers now. Generals. Captains. Every day more."

"Why, I think it must be . . . It is!"

Joab. Armor polished. Sword handle jutting like the bone on a mink. His armor-bearer at stiff attention behind him, ready to feed three spears into the fast-throwing hands.

Joab folded his arms across his breastplate when King David approached. The gesture could have been taken either for a salute or an insolent refusal to salute.

"News from Jerusalem?" King David demanded crisply. "Or has the nice weather brought you out for a friendly inspection? I have some of that wine you like in my quarters."

"Absalom is in the field."

"Coming here?"

"I reckon if I could find you, he can find his way, too. Mahanaim is not that hard to locate anymore. Once you get across the Jordan, you pick up the racket. All roads lead to Mahanaim when David sleeps there. I saw a good bunch of soldiers drilling on my way. If I were you, I'd pull them in and bunch them up. A few pickets by the river would do as well with less risk."

Itai said, "We take'm on the riverbank. Let'm try to cross."

"Is the young man leading the host himself?" asked the king.

"Him and Amasa," Joab said. "Amasa is an old woman, I say it, though he is my cousin. You would do wrong to underestimate him, though. He is a stickler for drill. He has had months to get ready. Absalom . . . I taught him a few rudiments myself. Whatever else you may say of him, his chariot will be in the van."

"You told him to march with a following wind," the king said with a droll laugh.

"I taught him what I learned from you."

"And is the wind following him?"

"He has made himself mighty popular with them that like him. Vigor. Innovations like he promised. A good reputation for fair dealing, now that he has taken hold. Since Achitophel did the right thing, it's been pretty orderly back there."

King David's lids shuttered his eyes for a long minute. There was no smile when he opened them again. "He's been a long time coming," he said. With his mole Hushai destabilizing the government, he had bought the months he required.

"A long time."

The king scrutinized Joab's face with heavy concentration. The battered nose. The bulldog chin under its irregular bristles. The curious slant of his cheekbones, which gave an appearance almost of merriment to his fathomless eyes. The head with hair cropped too short to give an enemy a handhold.

"So have you," the king said. "You've been a long time coming over, Joab. What made you so sure I'd be glad to see you when you finally came?"

Joab winked.

Joab

◆

KING DID well not to trust me with his whole command. In his place, would I have trusted me at all?

The battle was going to be a pisser. Anytime you went up against Amasa you could be sure he would have every shoelace tied and grease on every axle. Amasa was a quiet man, and maybe he lacked a little in being able to inspire fear, but give him time, and he would work out discipline by other means.

These rabbits who had gathered themselves to King through the winter were, to my mind, no better than a rabble. They had a "cause" and that gave each and every one of them encouragement to go about matters in his own way. Put them against properly disciplined regulars and who could predict how they would behave?

I did my best. Almost the first thing I did was catch a baker's dozen of them for wheeling left when the command was right and hang them then and there. Left the bodies dangling all night by the road, and the ravens had torn them up shockingly when we marched by them toward the river.

Amasa would not do such a thing, which was to my advantage, canceling partly the inadequate time I had for training. So if I could, I meant to try shock. I would fling cavalry and foot right straight at him without parley. If his men held, I would veer oblique to come at Absalom's flank — provided my bumpkins had caught on to oblique.

All dicey, you see. In truth, I never went into a battle as unpredictable as this would be. And Absalom was the wild card. He was crazy enough to bust right through us, and if his men followed him in any substantial quantity, that would be that, and yours truly would be hanging with some others to feed ravens.

To give another part of the truth, I was so dubious on the key matter of morale that when King said he would lead the battle himself I gave a sigh of relief. It was beyond superstition — I would have been knocked out long ago if ever I trusted a superstition — that when he was up for it, King had a knack for combat I could not match. Some way of eyeballing the field and knowing what has to be the next move without wasting time at calculation. The magic of it was, at the best, his troops would seem to know what he wanted of them instantaneous, without waiting a command almost.

With King directing the divisions he had entrusted to Abishai, Itai, and me, I thought the balance wavered a hair in our favor.

It was not to be. When the people saw David ride out to place himself with banner at the head of the march, they all began to squeal: "King David to the rear!"

He went up in his stirrups, see, and threw his hand on high in a signal to go. It was almighty stirring, so they yelled even louder, "King to the rear! King to the rear!"

I saw him quail. It was not this foolish tumult that changed his mind or could have changed it. The God of Battle was with him that morning, as He had been in all the famous victories.

Today, the God of Battle had thrown him a challenge too tough even for him — that he should ride out with the host to kill his favorite son. So he backed off.

When it was settled with some confusion that he was to wait in Mahanaim for the outcome, he called us generals aside, Abishai, Itai, and me, for his only instructions.

He had but the one thing to say to us: *"Deal gently for my sake with the young man, my son Absalom."* That was King for you. Never a doubt about which side would have the triumph. A trick with his words to drive the stopper in the bottle.

Nevertheless, he had not got a clear, simple meaning through to Itai. Riding, the three of us, to the point of our divisions, Itai asked, "How we kill'm we don't kill'm?"

Abishai answered, "The king means, we will utterly destroy the soldiers of Absalom and Amasa, but try to take Absalom uninjured."

"Amasa?" Itai asked.

"Kill him," I said.

Itai saw he could communicate with me better than with my brother. So he wanted me to confirm if King meant what Abishai said he did.

"More or less. You kill everybody you can reach and leave Absalom to me. All right?"

"Yis. Kill."

It was in Itai's simple mind that we would kill them at the river where they would come across after us, having surely the advantage of numbers and confident they could brush us back wherever we chose to stand.

We came to the river by midmorning, and there was no sign of them. Abishai sent scouts across to see if they were lying in ambush on the far side, ready for us to try the crossing first.

Not hide nor hair did his scouts find. They reported only that the farmers of the region had skedaddled, knowing something bloody was in the making. The plains were empty as far as the mountains in the north and fearsomely quiet as we marched over them, save for the clank of our men-at-arms and chariots.

The sun was two hours past noon when at last we came on them. I whistled out loud as I saw where the young fellow had spread his battalions there on the choice high ground, waiting with a patience I had thought beyond his character. It was perfect terrain, awfully tough for us, unless we faked him out of it by a march to his flank threatening to cut off the Jerusalem road.

Well, he learned something from me after all, I said to myself. The time I gave him was not a complete waste.

◈

There is something chokes me up whenever I have come on kings who have taken the high ground in battle array. It is glorious to see them up there with their banners to the center, the color flapping in the wind and the gold standards mirroring the sun. It is like to see hawks or eagles on the jut of stone high in the mountains, and you want to kill them because they are so fine and free. And it will be all right if it goes the other way, too. It is a good thing battle is so awful, or we would come to care for nothing else.

"We go up and kill them now, yis?" Itai said as we started our war council.

"You start up that slope and they will come through you like shit through a sieve," I warned him.

Useless. I will not speak badly of any man who was killed that day, but the fact remains Itai had no more sense of tactics than a dog. Let him set his teeth in a grip, and he would hang on until you strangled him with his own guts, I believe. That is a good soldier. Also a dead soldier.

His vote was to go right up before the sun got lower in case it took us time to slaughter as many as there were. Abishai tried to reason with him. The clearer Abishai made his illustrations and explanations of the options we had available, the less Itai trusted anything he heard.

"Wait a minute," I told Abishai. "Itai knows the capacity of his own men better than what we could. If he says they can make the climb and hold the ground, I believe that might work. You and I will take the flanks, and when Itai engages them, we will lunge in and all three of us topple them down the far slope."

"But . . ." Abishai looked scared. Up until then he had maintained his confidence in his older brother's savvy, if not in much else. Now he thought he had two crazies to deal with, and he would have to extricate himself and command as best he could.

I gripped him by the beard and told him, "There is no way for us to settle it except by vote. If Itai wants to make the preliminary attack, I vote to support him on the lines I said." Still Abishai did not believe in it. He was most worried that with my grip on his beard I might take the shortest way to relieve him of command, brother though he was.

But, in truth, I had seen the way we were going to pull it off. Remember the story I had told Absalom about the two-headed snake? Attacked in the center, both its heads can whip in to bite the attacker. In this case Itai's division could do little but slow down Absalom's chariots with a pile of bodies up to ten deep. Into that carnage on midslope Abishai and I would bite while Amasa was holding back to assess. If I knew Amasa, he would know about the two-headed snake even if Absalom had let it slip from mind. I would draw Amasa a diagram. Not with a stick marking in the sand, but by where I brought down my troops and Abishai's.

"Not too close in," I cautioned Abishai. "Get up that nigh hill as far as you can on your flank, so when you see my shit-kickers come out from those red rocks, we will both have the advantage of a downhill canter, and we'll see how Absalom likes that when it comes his turn to take it."

Abishai was always good at visualizing the potential of ter-rain. Certainly he knew from how I pointed out the geography there was no way in the world we could come down in time to save much, if any, of Itai's division. He gave me a look like he couldn't believe I would set it up like this without explaining to Itai what was about to happen to him. But then he gave a sick nod and rode to his command.

"Go get'm now?" Itai said.

"Go kill'm."

"Which one Absalom?"

"Never mind," I said. *"For the sword devoureth one as well as another.* King knows that. I heard him say it one time."

"Plizz?"

"Just get up there and kill'm."

"Yis!"

◈

I saw Absalom had taken the bait. Down he came from his high perch, all in a swoop. It was glorious to see, with his chariot first off the mark, like you pull one stone loose and the avalanche begins. Crackety-boom they came down into the badly dressed ranks of Itai's climbers, and the infantry piling on for their share of the massacre. What a froth they made.

Glorious, but it wasn't war. Not as I know it.

Absalom should have taken more careful notes when he studied the principles in my back yard.

I saw it was as good as over when I pushed my division out of the rocks at just the proper elevation, for there came Abishai's, right on time as well.

Absalom

———◆———

It was Amnon's fault, Father. He shamed my gentle sister before the dogs of Jerusalem. What was I to do? You should never have blamed me for washing out Tamar's shame.

The chariot horses leap with the sting of his whip. There is a slam-bang roar of metal rims on stone and splintering brush. Legs spraddled to keep his balance and ease the jolting snaps of his spine. Downhill all the way.

A king ought to be fair, Father. Then I knew you could not be fair.

His horses have gone crazy in the shock and mélée as they hit Itai's line. Their lips are peeled back from long green teeth, as if they would bite out the throats of any creature trying to slow the furious charge.

Father . . .

Have gobbled and chewed a bloody hole through Itai's battalions. Wheel at a dead gallop to encircle the remnant.

. . . I am sorry it had to come to this.

Suddenly, he has no horses, no chariot. Absalom is crawling on the ground with all the speed he can make. The side of his face is scraped. His right arm buckles painfully. A little blood seeps into his eyes. Then, on his knees, he sees Joab's men swarm out of the red rocks. Still a quarter of a mile away, but coalescing rapidly into a perfect front of spears.

It was Achitophel's fault.

He catches the bridle of a battle-dazed mule. Finds strength in his left arm to hoist himself onto its back.

Hears the tortured breathing of the animal turn into almost human moans as he rides at full gallop into the woods that are his sanctuary.

Father, it was Achitophel's fault. It was Achitophel's fault, Father.

Joab

———◆———

WELL, KING himself had told me to take care of Absalom, hadn't he?

Itai was dead. Abishai had taken no wounds, but I was the one who knew King's concerns in the matter from years of "confidential responsibilities." What he could trust no other for.

While our mopping up was still very much in progress, the captains told me they had seen Absalom grab a mule and make off into the woods. With my spear-bearer and a few others, I went in to track him.

Terrible thick woods. I was not a quarter-mile into them before I saw I would do better to dismount and continue on foot. There were branches broke to right or left at certain points, where Absalom had crashed through. They added up, more or less, to a beeline.

But where is he headed? Where on earth does he think he can go this time? I had to ask myself.

After the troubles with his kid sister and killing Amnon, it had been sufficient to get over the border and waste a few years. As we know, the story had a happy ending that time.

To my understanding, the point about happy endings is once you've had one, don't fuck it up. Life certainly does contain happy endings. They are not permanent. Not unless you sit with them real quiet in some corner and sort of nurse them forever, amen. A happy ending is about the most fragile thing I know.

You can't argue Absalom had hung onto his happy ending. He had had a run of luck and then tempted it. Now it was all to do over again, with me to aid him as before. But you can't repeat. Let seven come eleven. Pretty soon the snake eyes are looking at you from the table where you rolled them.

Cheerful thoughts I didn't have as we picked our way on down among the huge tree trunks where that poor mule had torn the underbrush. It was getting darker, both from the coming of evening and the thickness of the treetops over our heads. I was beginning to think we might better retrace our way and circle the woods to pick up where he might have come out on the other side. A mule that's properly scared can keep an astonishing pace. Afoot, we were nowhere near as speedy.

Then I saw it, almost in my face at about eye level. A foot with the strap still holding a sandal on it. Next I saw the other foot. Bare.

I raised my sight into the foliage, and at just that instant, Absalom let out the breath he had been holding when he heard us coming. "It's you," he said, much relieved at first to recognize me.

Never before or since have I seen a sight quite like he made dangling there. He was not swinging from a branch by his hands or a strap of armor as will sometimes snag a trooper who tries to speed through woods that dense.

He was hanging by that powerful hair of his. His head of hair had lifted him clean off the mule's back as they went under a lower limb. It turned out later that one arm was broken. The other had got tired, I guess.

"Help me down," he said. "I can't get a purchase." Then, seeing me in no hurry to do that thing, he said, "Again, I'm ready to face my father. You won't see me flinch this time either, Joab."

When I still did not reply or give my men the sign to aid him, he made a funny sob and the feet dangling near my face began to flop like a fish that has been out of the water a while. I think he was trying to get his good arm up to take some of the weight off his hair.

"Really, this hurts like hell," he told me. As if I might not know it did. Then he made a sound like my grandson does when he wakes up at night afraid. "My scalp will tear off!"

To my judgment, he had quit talking to me by then.

But who do you talk to when you are scared of what nobody else can understand? To yourself, maybe, and that is why you should choose your language with extreme care.

My spear-bearer coughed. I interpreted him correct. It was too damned embarrassing that I could find no answer for that boy hanging there so strangely in the strange evening light of the forest.

When my man coughed once more, I turned on him brutal. "You trying to remind me of my duty?" I asked.

He lacked the courage to cough again or speak, but I could read his mind in his face, howsomever dim the light. No doubt what he would have done, had the decision been his to make.

"Give me them spears," I said. I took all three from his reluctant hand.

"All right," Absalom said. "I should have sent for you instead of Amasa. There's a lot I should have done different. If you'll be good enough to let me rest my feet on your shoulder . . ."

I said, "I told you to get your hair cut."

Then I gave him all three spears. Right in the liver.

Solomon

———◆———

I am the rose of Sharon, and the lily of the valleys.

Oh he was! Now he was! He certainly was.

Bathsheba had gone downhill all the while Absalom was king. She ate compulsively — lots of chowders — putting on the pounds as she worried that Absalom might have a long life and father many princes of his own.

When the good news came that he was dead, she dieted cheerfully for three long weeks. That helped some. Again she looked like a pudgy lily herself. A buxom rose.

Last Days
of King David

David

♦

YEARS AND years later — in the time of the plague the Lord sent to punish him for numbering the people — the penitent king of Israel was traveling across the country from the threshing floor of Araunah toward Canaan. The Lord had at least been explicit this time in communicating His will: Build Me a new altar on the threshing floor and We will see about slowing down this plague. You are getting a lot of blame for it. Maybe more than you can handle, and I am not through with you yet.

It was a good altar they had built there on the threshing floor. A wholesome place for it. The king had no reason to doubt the plague would soon be lifted, so he rode away on his mule fairly at peace.

He tired quickly, though. Half a dozen miles along the way he had to be propped in the saddle by men walking on either side. Soon his retainers called for a litter and carried him.

A giddy and seasick ride it was, too. The swaying of the litter on the shoulders of his bearers made the sky tilt and slide abominably in his field of vision. The sky was rosy besides — not at all its normal Mediterranean blue. Treetops, palm and pine, swam like undigested vegetables in the puke color of the heavens. A cherub with disgusting breath peered into the litter from time to time, grinned, and soared back up into the stifling wind.

There was a sound of distant thunder. The king's bearers evidently took it for the beat of a military drum and syncopated their gait to its erratic rumbling. Brace himself as best he could on the litter cushions, the king was never quite prepared for the next lurch.

Ah, he was very sick. Sin crawled in his aging gut like a rodent turned loose to chew him from the inside out. His urge to throw up was controlled only by fear that he might drown in his own vomit. Common men might die of the plague they endured for his sins. His punishment was that he must ride this horridly bouncing coffin of luxury past graves old and new.

Then, when his procession seemed to have come among some lion-colored hills, the nausea was remitted. The landscape colors were still far from normal. The green outline of cedars was still bordered in red. The faces of his company were bright as saffron. But he felt the beginnings of recovery. He breathed with less difficulty.

Here he rapped on the side of the litter and commanded a halt. He commanded his shaky legs to hold him upright as he climbed out to stand on his own feet.

He looked around him approvingly. "What is this place? Where have we come?"

A captain who had ridden anxiously beside him said, "Milord king, to this day the people call it Absalom's Place."

"Why?" he asked with a thrill of surprise and foreboding.

"Look." The captain pointed to a naked escarpment and the

graceless, unfinished column that rose from it. "King Absalom had it built here."

It remained a disturbing structure, large, maybe a hundred feet tall with a top of irregular blocks where the builders had abandoned their work. It was too far from a city or village to have been intended as a monument. It had nothing in common with tomb architecture. The most disturbing thing about it, in fact, was that it gave no evidence at all of what its architect had in mind. It only stood there like a stone finger raised to invisible lips in a signal to hush. Or like a wrist with the hand amputated for daring to reach at the sky.

"Absalom set it here?"

"He did, milord."

"Do they say why?"

"The story is he built it because he had no son to keep his name in remembrance."

"He had . . . no son."

"Therefore he called the pillar by his own name." As he had named his abandoned girlchild for his shamed sister.

"Absalom!"

The percussion of the king's grief drove the captain to his knees. No man in the company could have looked then at the face of the bereaved lord. One by one the soldiers began to kneel. Then all were down except the king.

He held himself on his feet while his bones shrieked for capitulation. He fought the pull of the ground, wanting only to fling himself down and dig in for comfort. No enemy had ever wrestled with him like the tug of his hope for death and forgetfulness. He lamented the day when it had been said: There is a manchild born in the House of Jesse.

Yet he could not evade this long-promised torment of revelation. The iron nail of necessity tore through flesh to impale his soul.

Again he cried out in a main voice, "Absalom!"

The pillar stood against the lavender evening, mute, invulnerable to grief, lofty, not to be swayed by remembrance or forgetfulness either. It was stone and nothing else.

They called it Absalom's Place for its silence without an echo.

"My son, my son. Would God I had died instead of you."

He stood amid his kneeling retinue to watch the darkness climb stone by stone on that monument of futility until there was only a hair-thin edge of light on the unfinished blocks at the top. Then nothing.

◈

Those who watched with him and heard him cry out were never the same afterward and the world they lived in was never as substantial underfoot. They said — when they dared recall the episode — they had heard God wailing across the universe for a Son squandered by the implacable nature of things.

What they had heard was, at least, the belated utterance of a wail stuck in the king's throat since the evening Cushi brought news of Joab's victory. If his natural sorrow had poured out then, at the right time, it might have saved him. Considering the tasks ahead, surely he would have come back a better king after the full purgation for his loss.

It had been Joab then who slapped him out of it and denied his heart.

Yes, Joab had raised his fist against the anointed. Backhanded him across the room in Mahanaim until he yielded and did what Joab said was necessary.

"We gave you a victory and you shame us," Joab had roared in his bull rage. "Are we dogs you send hunting for your sport? Are we actors playing war to puff up your emotions? I was there. You ducked it. I was at Rabbah when you did in the Hittite to get his woman. I saw the Hittite take the blow he was

born to get. Do you think I couldn't piss and moan for Absalom? If I was an old woman, I could whine like you.

"I was *there*," Joab said. "Have you forgot that steel is steel
and fire is fire and everything hurts when they take it? Stand up
and answer me!"

"Now see here!"

"I said stand up."

When he could not, Joab jerked him by the beard. Got him
on his feet.

"There are your people out there in the street who think we
made a victory over Absalom and you are king once more. They
think you wanted it that way and you got it. If they hear you
whining, what has been won? I tell you, you went too far to
chicken now.

"I will not let you shame Absalom. He came down on us like
an eagle. Like a king. He was king and he is dead and you are
going to follow him. You are going to give him his place in the
line of kings if I have to beat you to save it for him."

Then, for once, Joab's guarded eyes were naked. There was
a flash of dreadful sympathy between the two men in which
David not only saw what his harsh servant was ready for but
wished with a kind of love to warn him against. *It is death to
strike the anointed.*

Joab did it anyway. Knuckles across the face, drawing no
blood, but driving the message bone against bone so it could not
be gainsaid.

"You will go out there. And you will tell them you are king
again. You will shout hurrah. Dammit, you will be king for
those who died and the rest of the sorry motherfuckers, or . . ."

Joab hit him again. With the same reckless, inexcusable force
of the first blow. A lesser king than David would have gone
down under that fist.

With blood under his beard, he went out to the people

massed in the street. He flung up both arms in the gesture
Moses made at the border to the Promised Land. There will
always be a promised land as long as there are kings to promise
and wretches unhappy with what they have got.

At his appearance, torches dipped and flared. The uneasy dis-
cord of voices smoothed and swelled into a limitless roar of
faith. The people chanted their victory and began to dance with
one another. The king had had a great fall. Now he was mended
and as good as new. Stuck together again with the glue of
popular demand, he watched it begin to happen in a daze of
wonder. The joke was on him after all. The Author of jokes
was as sly as ever.

◈

That turning point, his appearance to rally the people in
Mahanaim with a show of thanksgiving, was not one of his
great performances. Truly he would have to work up his act
when the time came to re-enter Jerusalem. He had barely managed to get his people marching on the road back.

And altogether the return to the capital was slow enough.
The spoils to be claimed by the victor were not exactly spilled
at his feet. On the roundabout junket back to the throne, he hit
many a small town, with politicking to be done at every layover.

The cranky populace had underestimated their fondness for
young King Absalom until he was dead. Those who had wished
in secret or in local caucuses for King David's restoration remembered now it was they who had anointed Absalom. They
argued *now* that the reasons for electing him must have been
powerful. (I reckon if *I* reasoned that way, it must have been
a good reason for it, you see.) The poison of democracy could
be dipped from every well where the fractious people gathered
to listen and be heard.

Let Royal David come tell us what he can do for us that Royal Absalom didn't have underway. The chief legacy of Absalom's revolt was that it gave folks the idea they could — should — pick their king, or even pick themselves to be the monarch of the moment.

All David's luxury of supposing that in his later years he might be a more spiritual king was abandoned on the far side of Jordan, made ridiculous when the old split between Judah and the other tribes had to be swaled with cornpone politics, pure and simple.

A little dealing with the priests Zadok and Abiathar: Go tell the elders of Judah the train is leaving the station and they better get on board. If the elders want to keep mouthing off, go straight to the tax gatherers. The tax gatherers will put some fire under them if they want to go on handling the boodle.

And the most delicate of all the requisite grossness was his somersault on the reorganization of the military. The conventional wisdom was that Joab, beyond question, was in line for the top job as well as for commendations and a special medal or two. Leaving aside all questions of loyalty and rebellion (if you could, in your confidence that you were betting on a sure thing), Joab had whupped Amasa in the field. The underdog had come out on top where it surely counted.

Imagine the shock, then, when the patched-up king calls a gathering of notables and gives the command to Amasa.

"Hear this: as long as David is on the throne, Amasa will command the hosts of the Lord."

Well! Now!

"Reckon you were as surprised as the rest of us, warn't ye Joab?"

"King has his reasons."

"Come on now. Warn't ye even a little bit surprised?"

"I didn't hire on to be surprised. Or not surprised."

"What ye gonna do now, Joab?"

"Old soldiers never die. Reckon I'll put my hand to writing my meemwars. Sit in the shade and whittle."

Even his good old wife is baffled by the calmness with which he takes the news. "Now I guess I'll have you underfoot *all* the time. Tell me, though, didn't it put your nose out of joint even a little bit to be passed over by him as well?"

"My nose? My nose, my nose, my nose, my nose." The old battler puts his hand on the organ in question, feels it with conscientious inquiry. "Oh, my *nose.* That's been out of joint since I can remember. What's for supper?"

Joab's brand of piety includes the principle that it is a mistake to slug your king, even as a favor.

◈

Glued together so the fractures only appear in certain slants of light, David would continue as king of "all the people," remarkably including those who spat on him when he was down.

He had hardly crossed back over Jordan — with Abishai as bodyguard — when they encountered Shimei once again.

The man had trimmed his beard and washed his face since their ruckus on the mountain. He had put on clean clothes — the better to make a show of dirtying them when he crawled on his belly and tried to lick King David's travel-soiled foot. (Get a mouthful, Shimei, and let's see how it sweetens your tongue!)

While Shimei groveled, the king kept his eyes level so he could count what Shimei brought with him besides an appetite for shit. A thousand good, tough-looking soldiers is what he brought. Beyond that (you can calculate fast when the whole election is hanging in the balance), these men and Shimei's

relatives were the core of the House of Saul. Feuds going back
to the beginning of David's reign could be tempered and con-
tained with Shimei on the team.

It was almost too much for Abishai. "Let me kill him *now*,"
he pleaded while Shimei was still down there wagging his bot-
tom like a dog who has found carrion. "I should have done it
when he cursed you." He shuddered to remember the foul
names.

As far as name-calling goes, Abishai, never get in a pissing
match with a skunk. Figure how to make him stop pissing.

"No, Abishai," said Royal David. "For the kindness done me
in my youth by Saul, I will bear no malice to Shimei. Nor any
of his men. Charity and justice for all. Bind up the nation's
wounds is the way I would put it. Is it not enough to know that
this day I am again king of all Israel?"

And he lifted Shimei to his feet. (Gave him a little pomegranate juice to wash the taste out of his mouth, you bet.)

"Yes, Abishai," he said in private to Joab's smoldering brother.
"Of course, Shimei will have to pay. I'll save you the privilege
of making sausage out of him. But not now. When the time is
ripe. Now we must not give way to rash feelings."

◈

A fancy messenger came riding to the king's tent to deliver
felicitations from Jerusalem. He presented a little vellum scroll,
inscribed by a most artistic and faithful hand:

> *For, lo, the winter is past, the rain is over and gone;*
> *The flowers appear on earth; the time of the singing of birds*
> *is come, and the voice of the turtle is heard in our land.*
> Welcome back, Dad.
>   Signed: Solly

The scroll had been scented with spikenard and myrrh.
So was the scroll that came by the next post from Bathsheba:

By night on my bed I sought him whom my soul loveth;
I sought him, but I found him not.
                          Signed: Thine

King David had heard from some professor or other that you could tell first-rate verse from wastepaper by its ambiguity. Sniffing and comparing the perfume on the two manuscripts gave him one level of meaning. The similarities of style and sentiment yet another. Why, you might almost take them for different stanzas of the same poem, mightn't you?

Another gratifying level of meaning lay in the metonym alluding to the voice of the turtle. Read that how he would, the king kept thinking how much like a turtle Shimei looked when he came crawling. And nothing sounds as sweet as really abject apology. That made it go nicely with the flowers and singing of birds in previous lines.

There were going to be some jolly good spots on the road ahead.

Abishai

———◆———

COMING UP the street past Joab's wall, I heard the sound. At the front door, Joab's old woman said he was out back under the trees.

"I know," I said. "I could hear him." I thought the sound was the way he would whistle if he ever whistled.

"Go right on through. He'll be glad for a visitor," his woman said. She is the meekest creature on earth, and if they ever lie down together, it must be like the lion and the lamb. Still, I believe she knows everything he is and has done and has made her peace with it. She would be the only person I can think of who is not afraid of him.

Though he is my blood brother, he scares me more than anything I can imagine, more than hurricanes or fire. From boyhood on I have sometimes stood up to him, but only when I was more scared of what he would do if I left him to his own intention.

That morning, he was standing to his grindstone, sharpening

a blade, and that is the sound I heard in my approach. As he noticed me come through the spotted shade under his fig tree, he held the blade up to squint down its edge. Then he put it to the wheel again. It was not one of his swords but a knife that bobbled on the grind wheel like a bright fish trying to escape his hands.

When the sound of grinding died again, I plunged right to my topic. "I have never heard you speak your side of the matter, but I believe I know why you felt right to kill Abner."

He looked satisfied now with the edge he had given the blade. He put his thumb on it and grinned cheerily. "Abner was a long time ago, brother."

I said, "It is enough for me that he killed our brother Asahel for running in pursuit of him when the battle was declared over."

Joab said, "There are many who give me that motive, yes."

"Nothing comes ahead of brothers. If blood will not take care of its own, then nothing at all will stand."

He nodded as if he had never thought of this before. Was glad I had said something useful.

"Amasa is our kin," I said. "If not brother, still cousin."

"He surely is."

"Whatever motive you had for Abner would not apply to Amasa."

He had to agree with that. But his thumb went again to the edge of his knife and it was more like he was in serious conversation with it and what I said was only on the fringe.

After a time, while I listened to his bees humming, he remembered I was present and said, "There are others suppose I did King's business to eliminate Abner. If he was not yet become a traitor, in time he might have."

"Well now," I said. "Anyone *might* be. You can't go about eliminating one and all for what they *might* do."

"It would be a vast undertaking."

"You didn't raise a finger when King Absalom put Amasa up ahead of you to lead the host."

"That's true," he said. "I didn't."

"Then you will not go for him now?"

"Would you give me the motive of jealousy? I am getting on in years. I am jealous of no man, nor covet what is rightly theirs."

"Do you think the king did right and fair to give him the command when you had proved better in the field?"

"Look, brother," he said. "This is a mighty serious matter you have got on your mind. The kingdom is still terrible stirred up. King has set Amasa to be in charge of the host for any fighting which is necessary now. You are thinking about King's own appointed leader of the host being killed. I recommend you should take this serious matter to King himself."

He was not breathing hard or showing any emotion as he said this. I was. "No," I said, "I will not take it to the king. It is a matter of our family, our blood, and if it cannot be settled on such grounds, I have no hope. Amasa's mother, who is our mother's sister, came to me, and . . ."

"I thought maybe she would."

". . . wanted me to beg you. So I am begging."

He did not show me any contempt for saying so. It was more that he seemed satisfied I had used the right word between brothers, and he approved me. "I see she knows me well," he said. "She is a good woman."

"Then?"

"Don't tell her nothing. She is a good woman and had a right to send you to me. That is as far as her rights go. I have listened to you and given you my advice to take it to King. That is as far as I will answer."

"I should not have brought up Abner," I said.

"No, you should not."

"Since I don't know what was between you and the king on him, nor on our cousin Amasa. I think you will do what is necessary."

"That's right," Joab said. "I couldn't promise you or any man more than that."

❖

So what is treason?

I admit I don't know, though beyond any question a soldier will have to deal with it the only way he can when it appears. Deserters must be savaged and thrown to the dogs. Traitors must be hung when possible. That is the way of it, and I would no more question it than the sun rising.

The mystery is in the timing. You cannot always count on hanging a traitor after his treason, for the chances are always good that by then he has hung or otherwise disposed of you. If you hit your man on the mere possibility he might be disloyal, you could quickly run through your whole army. It is a riddle for kings and one prime reason I would not bear them envy.

It is a riddle that kings do not like, which is why they all must have someone like Joab. To go right into the darkest part of the mystery and strike blind. My brother was the stone King David flung when he had need to kill two birds. I would make a poor substitute for that.

❖

When King David called me to him, there was treason boiling all over the place. I would not say most of it was in his own mind, though it jolted me to the bone to see the grand king so near hysterical.

I had come to the palace thinking it might be time for me to stretch a rope with Shimei. I was up for that, for the case seemed fairly simple. The term of the contract had come round and that was that, I thought.

"Shimei?" King David said in his shrill voice. "He is the least of my worries. Or maybe he is in on it too. By all means hang him. Have you got him where you can do it?"

I admitted not knowing his whereabouts since he had risen from crawling on his belly.

"You see? As things are going since my return, no one will stay put. I suppose you don't know where Amasa is either."

"I do. He has left the city to assemble the men of Judah."

"That's not an answer, that he has left the city. Of course he has. He went on my orders. Went out of sight. Why did I ever trust someone who had such a big part in the rebellion?"

"Amasa would be very loyal," I said, thinking that if he had dropped from view while on legitimate business, the real question ought to be where was Joab.

"Would be, would be," King David wailed. "Anything is possible. The fact remains he is not here when I need him most. Sheba is our foremost problem. I mean that son of Bichri."

It was coming too fast for me, though I got the gist. Sheba had picked a red-hot moment to blow his trumpet and call Israel to follow him. Which a great pack of them had done, not so neat as when Absalom took over, but still a first-rate mess. They were massing over around Abel and had been in position to fortify several other cities because there was no Amasa to lead the remaining troops to prevent it.

"For all I know when Amasa gets the men of Judah formed up, they will circle around to join with Sheba. So you will have to strike before that can happen."

Me? His offer was that I should command the host. What was left of it.

"Milord king," I said, as sincere as ever in my life, "since Faithful Amasa has not returned, why not restore Joab to the post that some feel he deserves?" It was my one big try at diplomacy. If successful, it would remove from Joab the temptation to go directly after Amasa. I also had some compunction against finding the knife in my own back should I succeed in the commission I was being offered.

"Joab? Joab hates me," King David said. It would have been political, maybe, to deny this outright, but I feel safer close to the truth.

I said, "You are his king."

That grabbed him. A kind of crafty, meditative expression settled his face. He stopped grimacing and managed a long, steady look deep in my eyes. "Yes," he said, "I am Joab's king. I must not forget what manner of man he is. And I see you are of the same breed. I am your king, and I order you to take the host, go settle Sheba. Destroy him before he pinches off any more cities. Destroy Sheba and you will have Amasa's place permanently. As long as David is on the throne, Abishai will command the hosts of the Lord."

"Just for this one campaign," I said. He had winkled me so I could no longer refuse outright what he wanted when he summoned me.

"No, no, no, no!" he said. "You will be my commander and sit at my right hand. How about wives? A man in your position will need some showy wives as time goes on. I have a couple of first-class daughters coming up to the right age, hey? We'll discuss the trimmings when you come back. Just bring me Sheba's head and you'll never need to ask again for suitable perks. I believe you know the saying: Rank has its privileges."

I was meditating the risks. "I still say Joab." I remembered Joab had offered to let me run my thumb on the edge of that knife he was honing. I had said no, thanks.

"Oh, take Joab along with you on the campaign," King David said with much-improved humor. "For good luck. To make faces at Sheba when you've caught him. Ha ha."

I said I would rather not.

◈

It was an uneasy march when we went on to deal with Sheba. The troops and the mighty men went sullenly. With so much treason loose in the country, me new in the command, and all preparations so hasty and jerry-built, why should they have confidence?

It didn't help the men or me to note that Joab came along after all, dressed as a common soldier and footing it along in the ranks, carrying his own spear. I was so put out to mark him there that I rode right past him without as much as a nod.

The first day's march was hot for that time of year, with rotten-looking clouds toward sundown dimming what little spirits we had managed to keep up during the early hours. When I gave bivouac orders, the captains began a chatter of questions about the lay of the land where I meant to make camp. We had sent out scouts to look for hostiles in the gullies of that place, and most of them had not come back. I was persuaded they deserted back to Jerusalem, or maybe found the enemy and gone over without further ado.

In my depression, I sent for Joab to be brought to my tent. Not to advise me. I knew well enough he would recommend having the men draw straws, then string up the lads who drew the short ones so the rest would be gung ho in the morning.

He came in and saluted smartly.

I asked, "What's the meaning of this? At your age, playing at being soldier."

"Sir, I have kept up with the march."

"I meant being dressed like a shitkicker and toting your own spear."

"Everyone knows who I am, sir." He didn't shrug as he said it. That would have been unmilitary, given my rank.

"Why'd you bother to come along at all if you only mean to sulk?"

"King sent me," he said, showing a little bit of tooth.

"What for?

"Maybe it's the Uriah play. Did he give you a letter 'Put Joab in the forefront of the hottest battle and retire from him that he may die,' sir?"

I replied with some heat that I would never do so and he knew it. "I do know that, little brother," he said.

"So that's how he got rid of Uriah, was it?"

"How *we* got rid of Uriah. I don't have the scruples you do. That's what got me where I am today."

"Letter or no, I'll put you up front if that's the way you want it."

He took my beard in his hand and drew me to him for a fond, brotherly kiss. "You'll make out fine, Abishai. You're a good lad. Just do what King wants and you'll go a long way."

Then we went outside together to watch by the campfire until it dimmed. He told me all he knew about Uriah and Bathsheba. It still amused the hell out of him, and as he told it, strangely it did not seem disrespectful of King David.

◈

With the morning came another complication. There in the stifling air, just as the baggage wagons were loaded and we were breaking camp, who should show up, in full regalia, but Amasa himself.

Of course he wasn't a traitor at all. Had been held up longer than expected in the towns over near the River Jordan, that was all. The people of Judah needed some stroking and cajoling to line them up. But all was now well on that front. We could proceed against Sheba without a fear of disintegration behind us.

As soon as word had come to him that Sheba had stirred up trouble, Amasa had called out his personal guard and headed back to assume command. Had ridden all night and was glad to find he was in time to do his duty.

Dusty as he was from the hard ride, he looked every inch the chief as he came striding toward my tent there by the great stone of Gibeon. He had a big feather in his turban. The gold chain of his rank was doubled around his neck. The jewel-handled sword I remembered from Joab's wearing it was in the sheath that swung smartly against his thigh. The troops gave him a cheer. I could see this would be a different day from yesterday, and the whole truth is I was glad to see him there to relieve me.

He kissed me on both cheeks and thanked me for filling in "so well" until he came back to his proper spot. We were still in this cousinly embrace when he said, "Ah!" He had seen Joab over my shoulder.

"Joab came along to advise on strategy," I said.

"Splendid," said Amasa. "Another omen of success. With him at my side, how can I fail?"

He called Joab by name, very friendly, and almost practically skipped across the sand to give him the kind of hug he greeted me with. Only, somehow — and it was like black magic, I swear — as he bounded off, that jeweled sword popped right out of its sheath and almost tripped him up in falling.

I thought he was embarrassed to drop his sword right there in front of the army, after his talk about omens. So, instead of stopping to pick it up, he kicked it away and hurried to take Joab in his arms.

Joab gave him a bright smile and seemed to bow a little.

Gracious, and still playing that he was not of officer grade. He took hold of Amasa's beard in the same fond way he had tugged mine the night before when I was low. With his other hand he put the steel into Amasa's back.

Ripped him all the way around, so Amasa's bowels were spilling onto his sandals before his mind could tell him to lie down because he was dead.

◈

Some spectacles will turn any man to stone. Though, as I have told, this killing had passed through my mind, I was not expecting it now. It was done in one of those minutes that has nothing to do with time. There is a before and an after, but that minute is like a painted picture that may last to eternity but has no duration or connection with present time.

What was *after* was Amasa lying there in his guts and military regalia, bleeding enough so he might have floated himself away, while one of Joab's old sergeants is already shouting, "Whoever is for the king, let him follow Joab!"

I was far from the only one who was petrified while the deed was done. Believe that our whole army was stone. If Sheba's people had come on us then, they wouldn't have had a battle. They could have pushed us over from vertical to horizontal and left us lying.

Yet — such is the nature of war and the men who make it — the paralysis ended as abruptly as it came on us. A shout went up and echoed over the ranks. It was in no way a lament for Amasa. The opposite.

"Joab! Joab! Joab!"

You could hear it spread over the rough hillocks and up the gulches where the troops had been preparing to move out. And then, soon, we had left the rough terrain, marching in swift columns with the chariot horses neighing and the foot soldiers up on their toes in a trot.

There could not have been imagined a greater reverse from what the army had been when it slunk out of Jerusalem. The cherubims of victory swept the air ahead of us, and now Sheba never had a chance.

We took his head back soon to King David in Jerusalem. There was little argument afterward, for years to come, that Joab was the proper leader of the host.

Solomon

◆

Ennuyant!

Without happy dust from Nineveh, how could one endure the boredom of Sabbath afternoons? Then all my diversions are smothered by the sheer dead weight of existence. My personality becomes a straitjacket within which the self wriggles, trying to get at an itching nose. The cosmos crouches motionless on leaden foundations. All living creatures sense the nausea of this meaningless inertia. My pet lemurs, Whoopee and Clitoris, are sad.

I begin to understand the attractions of warfare and fornication — for others, I mean.

Hypothetically, war is the sovereign remedy for boredom. Some higher natures seek it by the same kind of instinct that leads animals to salt. The masses, to be sure, know little of boredom and are not, in the main, enthusiastic about going to the wars. They have to be seduced to carnage by juicy stories of atrocity or the promise of homecoming parades. For the philoprogenitive, civilization with its discontents is sufficient to their being.

Boredom is the king's evil. (Have I not understood the pater after so much intense scrutiny? In his penultimate years, he scratches for enemies like a sleepy dog going for its fleas. Hopefully, irritably, and at last feebly. He has given up on wars as he lapses into the boredom of dying.)

With my equivocal gift of empathy, how could I not perceive how the itch for war lurks in the matted fringes of a brain no longer virile? History can be no consolation for such a spirit, with its cursed orientation toward things still to come. Nothing has ever enchanted him like *what is about to happen next.* Go take a hundred foreskins from a fresh generation of Philistines! Drive the Syrians like antelope in their mountains! Strike north to chastise the impious Greeks! Pre-empt the poor Ammonites who have so often served as his punching bags in days gone by! Burn the tents and baggage. Butcher a thousand and show mercy to ten thousand.

I glimpse, too, the signal ecstasy of showing mercy after slaughter.

He even revives his old plans to build, at last, a suitable temple here in Jerusalem. Calls on me to review the sketches and, I suppose, to admire his taste.

In all candor, I must say his architectural conceptions are those of an amateur and, alas, a country boy. A temple of cedar, indeed! That might make a nice addition to the "skyline" of Bethlehem. It is totally inappropriate for the New Jerusalem. Baal and Belial would have the horse laugh on our Lord to see Him housed in architecture that I have labeled Log Cabin Contemporary. Understandably, our congregation would yearn for heathen splendor.

Nathan "approves" this talk of temple-building. Need I say

more? As long as the Temple has seminar rooms in the basement where Nathan can lecture our youth on social questions and give them utterly farcical sex education, never mind the effect of the ensemble. Even cedar might strike that disguised Philistine as a diversion of funds that ought to be used in soup kitchens.

The New Jerusalem will only arise when . . . But never mind. It is too *ennuyant* altogether to rehearse in full sobriety the dreams unfolded for me by the angelic poppy.

◈

In the pater's great days, copulation was second only to warfare in his majestic struggle with boredom. How do I know this? Aha. A flock of little birds told me! One particular little bird among them, to be sure. Oh, Bathsheba. The Fair Bathsheba. How droll she is in her euphemisms and circumlocutions! How solemnly (Solomonly) I always listened to her recollections of his "manliness" urged to its peak by the incandescence of her "charms." Translated into hard-core pornography, her book would conquer the known world, I do believe.

Alas, for her beloved son, it is consistent comedy, and I write of copulation with the same melancholy *au fond* as of the martial arts. Neither is for me. Since those boyhood days when I experimented with puppies, kittens, and little sparrows, I have admitted I could not joy in bloodshed. Bashing out brains left me unmoved. (Correction: *insufficiently* or *inappropriately* moved.) The aesthetics of blood or of vital tissue in disarray are no more accessible for me than is music itself. The featherless sparrows I crushed turned my stomach permanently. Of the other animals, I merely felt: good riddance. A servant might have disposed of them for all it mattered to me. A warrior is not made of such stuff.

As for copulation, it would be the crown of existence — did it not involve the total physicality of another person. If women were indeed as they appear in erotic fantasy, then even the New Jerusalem would be too poor a habitation. I adore their shape, their motions, and the eternal play of nuanced light on their skin. If women could only be skindeep, no more! If one could only *foutre* them from a distance of, say, fifteen to twenty feet . . . ! Unfortunately they have entrails, the entrails secrete astonishing reminders of mortality. At puberty, when the word *cunt* was for me a magic incantation and summons to worship, a disaster occurred: I saw one.

An enamored maid was going to do me a favor. Give up her flower to the panting young prince. Prepared me. Prepared herself. I opened my eyelids, expecting to look at the very center of my idealistic yearning and . . . Too bad, too bad.

Landscape — that is to say nature — has an intermittent appeal. Yet not this blatant landscape of Israel with its abundance of light. Twilights and dawns are my soul's *milieux. Je suis le roi d'un pays de pluie.* Oh, give me the splendid mountain fogs of the land beyond the wind, and I might for once know myself at home! To be fogbound while *yearning* for the sun — is that not to be far happier than to have the sun delivered every day like a loaf of bread from an uninspired baker?

Without royal blood (and B's importunate ambitions to be, in fact, *mère du roi*), I might have been, even here, a happy gardener. An architect of blossoms! Floral arrangements are among my accomplishments that might have burgeoned *in excelsis* with proper encouragement.

Yet the nagging truth here (you see how I strain to present my heart most nakedly) is that I cannot take in hand a lily, for example, or a rose, or even a pomegranate, without wondering how it might be wrought more perfectly in glass or metal.

I find no remedy, then, for my *douleurs* except the very local palliative of art.

And the excruciating dilemma is that art requires funding.

(*Hypocrite lecteur,* did you not know that funding was the soul of art?) Art on the scale of my best conceptions requires nothing less than the whole treasure of the region. From Egypt to Mesopotamia. Basalt, beryl, chalcedony, pearl and mother-of-pearl, bronze and marble veined with bloodless blue and pink. Carvers from the delta, craftsmen slaves from Damascus, masons from Babylon.

The New Jerusalem can only rise when we have demolished the hovels and have laid out radiating boulevards with monuments at the city limits. Aqueducts for a thousand fountains. Everywhere an alternation of greenery, flowers, and well-wrought brass.

The temple I have conceived shall be twenty cubits in length and overlaid entire with gold. A partition of gold chains will segregate the oracle, and carvings of cherubim in palm trees will be the posts of the house, and on the folding doors will be open flowers, wrought in odorous woods and inlaid with many gems.

❖

All that — while in the vexation of reality I practice chiefly the art of patience, be my yearning as impatient as Brother Absalom's. Patience, watchfulness, an exile in the house arrest of my own bosom, and . . . *the scrutiny of women!*

Women, as I have divined them to be, are not as boring as they intend to make themselves by their endless preoccupation with love, marriage, and bearing children — as if the grip of reproductive nature held them in perpetual thrall.

Even in these lower aims they teach something. One studies their debased arts as one studies the aim of highest art in their astonishing physiques. In my vocation as *migliore fabbro* (Do you take this for immodesty, reader? Have I deceived you by protestation of *modesty*?) I adore the exterior of the female body, or bodies in multiples, as they *appear* to transform sensuality into immortal form. I adore the spectacle of nature straining to transcend itself in the beauty of women. I watch them from my secret places in breathless dread, wondering sometimes if, even yet, I may trust my ecstatic flesh to their ardors. Nathan suspects me of "secret vice" and his nagging must sometime be challenged.

But his vocabulary is not mine. For me, the vistas of erotic language open on a more luxuriant paradise, as I stalk patiently down a path whose ways were *ab initio* dictated by Bathsheba.

Beyond any peradventure of present doubt, my mother is index and codex for my communion with the female anima. How grotesque to remember that once upon a time B was simply "my mother." Depth psychology merely noodles with the role of female parent in the formation of the artist's nature.

Equally certain is that the transformation from "mother" to archetype began when I commenced to write about her. Properly explicated, my "Song" is seen to be a series of quite precise observations of B in her majestic absurdity, her moods, her changes. The "author" simply does not intrude in the verse except as recording *instrumentum*. Passions inspired, passions requited, are those of an almost cosmic (wholly comic) female self in erotic counterplay with its sensual projections.

Erotic totally — *therefore* B is a fusion of erotic, spiritual, and political themes. Surely a fit mother for a King of Kings. To ponder that out of this reginal cosmos came I! Only then do I comprehend my fitness for the throne.

In the meantime, what a wonder and what a loss if I should not prepare myself by continuing to study woman in all her manifestations.

How they are all the same! How each is unique!

There is a vulgar saying: They all split in the same place, don't they? (A serviceable variant for *la nuit tous les chats sont gris.*) A truth never to be neglected by the researcher. A truth never to be stretched beyond its limits of usefulness.

Infinitely the same, my doves, my *chats.* Infinitely different — as though each were part of the limitless dream of all. Their individuation is not the same as the individuation of men. So, the mere male who aspires to art will toil — where I must go when I am quite ready, often and again often — within the sheets where woman wrap their mysteries. Unwind the sensual cocoon, Solomon! Unravel thread by thread the precious strands from which cloth of gold will be spun to drape the New Jerusalem!

I will live to build it. I will. I will. Somewhere on the façade of my masterwork, I must encode the name Bathsheba. For of all things *ennuyant,* she continues to be least so.

◈

Look at the silly creature now!

Oh, she is not jealous. Oh never. Shocked, amused, concerned, apprehensive — anything you please, but certainly not jealous that "the virgin," Abishag, has been put in pater's bed.

"A *health measure!*" she cries in limitless scorn. "His poor old limbs are chilly! Of course he won't take care of himself properly, so who is surprised? And the so-called medical profession can think of no way to warm him but covering him with that insipid girl. Have you ever heard of such a thing?"

"It's the inspiration of genius," I pronounce. "Intercapillary heat exchange on the Framingworth Scale usually thromboses the hypercortal frangibility."

"You should have been a doctor, Solly. But . . ."

"It's absurdist theater of the most impudent and exquisite audacity."

"That's what I say. Absurd! Do you know what I actually suspect, Solly?"

To be sure, she suspects the worst. What she will conceive to be the worst among a vast range of possibilities always catches me by surprise.

"That he won't be able to?" I tease. "Or that he *will* be able to? Once the intercapillary phrebilia begins to work on him, I mean."

"Oh, he won't be able to," she says with a degree of assurance that makes me marvel. Through all the wives and concubines who have come and gone in my lifetime, B remains supremely confident that she alone has the true reading of his libidinous capacity. Her assurance provokes a fleeting smile of satisfaction. "Of course he won't be able to! But that in itself adds to the danger. Impotent old men try to make up for what they can't do by giving gifts. By submissiveness."

"I see. He'll set a big pearl in her navel. Harness her with gold. Well, he can afford it."

"His *ring*," she whispers theatrically. "The king's own ring. She'll try to get it off his finger."

"B, I just wouldn't worry about that. Even if he gave it to her and she came out wearing it, that wouldn't, by itself, make her the next king. As I size up the political landscape, Israel isn't ready for a virgin king."

"She may not be," B says, bearing down hard to get me to admit the seriousness of the crisis. "Suppose this Abishag isn't a virgin after all?"

"All the better for warmth."

"Don't make fun of me. You'll be sorry if you don't listen. It involves your brother Adonijah."

"Is he complaining of chills too?"

She shudders at the immorality Adonijah may have committed on this unworldly girl — or at the prospect Adonijah has made another bid to edge me out as next king. "Before the physicians selected her, I know it for a fact that Adonijah told someone she had 'the hottest hips in Hebron.'"

"Wheeew! A thermal miracle. Now I understand the drift of your thinking, B. You think Adonijah planted her to steal pater's ring and give it to him so he can claim the throne when . . ."

"When the worst happens."

"Well, Mums, what are we going to do to thwart this wicked plot?"

"I don't know, Solly. I tell you I'm worried half sick. That's why I came right to you. You're smarter than I am, and I hope you can think of something."

"What does Nathan say we ought to do?"

"Being so worried, I wanted to talk to you before I got his advice."

"Mums!"

"Yes. Well, he's just as baffled as I am. He went to your father with a parable as soon as he heard about it. Sickening! There was that creature lying *face up* right on top of your poor chilly father, shameless as you please. Poor old Nathan couldn't bear to look at the two of them. He told his parable . . ."

"About the care and feeding of sheep."

"Yes. And all your father had to say, from *under* this brazen hussy was 'Some sheep!!' What did he mean by that, Solly? 'Some sheep!'"

"It means there's life in the old boy yet. Neither Adonijah nor I need worry about replacing him for years to come."

She begins to cry and takes my hand to put it against her wet cheek. It is her old routine to remind me that the only wish of her motherly heart is to see me and my gifts properly recognized. Neither my verses nor my architectural designs will be fully appreciated if I linger in the shade. I was always her little king and it will break her heart now, at the finish line, if Adonijah crosses us up. Or if pater is poky about dying, I guess.

"Don't cry, Mums. I'll think of something. Mmmmmm. I haven't seen this fireball Abishag yet. She must be yummy, yummy."

"Her hair . . . has no body to it. It's limp and it's thin."

"Maybe in spite of her totally revolting hair I should waylay and ravish her. No, I'll give her some happy dust and ply her in the Grecian manner and get her to steal the ring for me. We'll hoist that crooked Adonijah with his own puny petard."

With B, I have kept up the pretense I have laid half the females in Jerusalem. That consoles her — she believes it is kingly.

Now she giggles and gives me a playful slap. "Solly, you've got to be serious."

She kisses me on the lips, and I promise I will be serious and come up with a solution.

◈

Abishag, Abishag, Abishag, Abishag, Abishag.

It strains your credulity, reader, to think of Wise Solomon in love?

Well, comfort me with flagons and stay me with apples, if I didn't fall in love at first sight.

Innocently enough (!!!!!!!!!!) I had made my way to the peephole that looks down into the women's bath with only a half-formed expectation that I would glimpse this innovation in medical science cleaning up for another treatment of my father.

Through the chink in the stones I scanned the whole harem in languid disarray around the tepid pool. Some were tickling lutes while others lolled back on their vivid cushions to listen. Some were playing a slow water game, not splashing so much as sending tremors and wavelets back and forth to each other, eyelids down and smiling at the secrets they communicated. Some were cuddling so their breasts met in soft collisions. As usual, there was more than one hard nipple in the flock. A raven-haired pythoness with a well-shaved mons was dancing in a shaft of sunlight that fell from the fenestrations under the roof beams. The quality of the harem, you see, has improved in pater's last years in inverse proportion to his flagging powers. *Vide* Solomon's Law:

$$\frac{\sqrt[3]{a}}{1} = \frac{\sqrt[3]{1}}{b}$$

Before I was jaded with autoeroticism, I used to come to this peephole for many devotions. Some of my loftiest themes were given to me here — verse, prose, and glimpses of monumental, breathtaking architecture — as I squeezed out my thrilling tributes to the principle of creation.

Yet — secret of secrets — I had not, I suppose, dared guess what I was meant to comprehend when I saw — so close, so far — the back of Virgin Abishag.

It is true I saw *only* her back that day when I fell in love. And it is just as true that I recognized her instantly — God ordained I would not have to see her features to know who she was and everything she might be to me.

She was sitting apart from the other women, on a stone block or chair not fifteen feet from where I knelt. She was immobile as a piece of sculpture. Yet that ruddy, olive torso seemed to wheel like an austere planet on its course among the merely sensual females of the bath. She had on her head some sort of white cloth or toweling, and from her right shoulder another white garment, or vestige of one, trailed down to the water-spotted floor. I do not remember all the dimples and curves of that sumptuous back (nor would I report them if I did).

I knew in a panic of unforeseeable knowledge that it was *the sun in me* she was orbiting in her planetary course.

With sublime certainty, I knew her body was virgin in the same rare sense that mine is. A virginity so often lost in the pulsation of fervid dreams that it was proof against any mortal thrust or tumble. That back was a mighty landscape where caravans and hosts of men might come to spill their seed without a hope of penetration. Stallions, boars, and rams might drench that smiling *corpus* in their lust. The lightest sprinkling of afternoon rain would purify her totally. I thought: Not even my father in his youth could have entered her. For she was the prize of my virginity as I was now the prize of hers.

If Abishag had turned then so I could see her face, I would have died on the spot. *I knew whose face I would see.*

I was reminded on the instant that this was forbidden knowledge. Yes, even as the ecstatic terror thrilled me, I heard old Nathan's phlegmy cough in my ear and felt the dampness of his spittle on my cheek. After all the years of stalking me, he had at last caught me here at the peephole, trembling like a child.

Like a king, I faced him down. "You pretend to honor wisdom, Nathan," I said. "Kneel here and look on it in its nakedness. For once, put your nose to the chink in the stones and behold if you dare."

I grabbed him by his dowdy hair and actually twisted him to his knees. I was advancing his face closer and closer to the aperture where beauty might have killed him . . . when I realized he had outwitted me by simply clenching his eyes shut. So I let him get up, sputtering.

"Hurry," he said. "Hurry. I've been searching for you everywhere. There's not a minute to spare. I must talk to you or all is lost."

I laughed then, but without contempt. Nothing was going to be lost. Nothing could be lost now that I knew the sun in myself. I knew I was the king whatever Adonijah's strategy might be. And I knew why B had been so afraid of Abishag.

Bathsheba and Abishag

◆

A WHISK AND a skip and bare-assed Abishag is out of the king's bed. Her pretty toes twinkle down the palace corridor to her own little room. Thank goodness a friendly concubine slipped by in time to warn her the Queen Mother was on her way.

How would you like to explain to the dowager that you were sleeping with King David on doctors' orders? His doctors' orders, that is, and her excuse would have sounded flimsy to her own ears if she were forced to stammer it out. Those old farts had taken their time examining her, poking and pinching and prodding to see if any of her cavities harbored disease (or were they looking for birds' eggs up there?) hefting her boobs and tickling her armpits most leisurely before they pronounced her fit to lie with the old king and *keep him warm*.

Hypothermia aggravatata. Poor old fellow was chilly all the time now. A nice healthy virgin to cover up with was the best prescription his physicians could devise. (Provided she still *was* a virgin after their examinations.)

The nicer part was the king had seemed grateful for the health benefit. She had been told you could count on older men for that, at least.

"Thank you," he said. Not a bit pompous or condescending to a country girl.

His lips were blue down under the snowdrift of his beard, and he had been shivering pitifully when she shucked her robe and crawled under his covers. So cold he made her shiver, too.

Then they were both shivering together, though it seemed a different kind of shivering after a few minutes. Men were men, however old and royal they might be. Partly, she was shivering to think that whatever she hadn't lost to the doctors, she was about to lose in a more natural manner. The old fellow still had *ideas*.

Then he said, "Thank you, anyway," and now that she could reflect on that in the safety of her room, she was a tiny bit disappointed, though probably lucky. It looked now that Prince Adonijah might get it after all, and though he was ten times the man his shriveled father had become, it would have been something to tell her girlfriend back home that King David himself had been there first.

So after her escape, she was atwitter with mixed yearnings. She wished with all her hot little heart she could be a mouse in the corner of the king's room to hear what Bathsheba might be saying. It could very well be about her, since now she remembered the telltale garment she had left beside his bed.

◈

"Chilly, darling?" Bathsheba asked.

"Mmmmmmmmnnnnn."

"What's that?"

"Yes and no."

"I brought you a nice down coverlet, because they told me you were shivering in the night." She fluffed the coverlet and let it settle atop the thick blankets already stacked on him. With thumb and forefinger, she picked a gleaming dark hair from the pillow beside his head. "The maids are so careless these days," she observed. "I'll have to speak to them about hygiene in the sickroom."

She saw the abandoned robe on the floor, kicked it under his bed unobtrusively, and sat down. The bed groaned under her weight. She outweighed any two of his younger women.

"If I get chilly again, I'll send for you," he croaked. Trying to cover his guilt as usual. And she would not deny him that vain exercise. What had she ever denied him that was good for him?

"I'm not very useful in that department anymore," she said. "Though we had some sizzling nights in the old days. Someone should keep all our memories in a book."

"The Bible?" he croaked.

"Oh David, really! You could always get a giggle out of me, even when I was most depressed. No, silly, I mean the real stuff. The 'goody part' you used to call it when you said your Bathsheba made up for all the trouble of being king at everyone's beck and call."

She thought she heard a sob.

"There, there," she said. "I didn't come here to bring painful reminders. What's done is done. But I want you to know this: If you were to find a younger woman, what you used to speak of as 'another Bathsheba' — and I thought that was a gallant way of putting it — I wouldn't say boo. I'd be glad. And if you sent for her in the night when you were chilly, I'd just keep my mouth shut. I mean this with all my heart."

Now his sobbing sounded really contrite. She was satisfied he had tried and failed with the little tramp who ran off without her robe.

"David, I came only because there's something serious to settle. Something we haven't discussed for too long. Besides to bring you the coverlet, I mean."

Grumble grumbled from his old blue lips.

"I can't hear you," she said.

"I said probably Solomon would make as good a king as any of them left around."

"Well, that's putting it pretty neutrally, I must say. I suppose they're still working on you to get you to change your mind, after you promised so often. David, you promised that our Solomon would sit on your throne. Deny that!"

She fished under the bed and produced Abishag's robe. "Deny this!" she challenged, shaking the cloth in his face. "And I know whose it is, too. Poor old man. Can't you see the trick they're up to?"

"Whose?" he asked feebly.

"That Abishag person Adonijah dug up and smuggled in here under some excuse or other. Deny that!"

"Abishag," he confessed.

"Oh, they know your big weakness. Rub it against the old boy and you can at least addle his mind and get his signature or steal his ring. Something they can use to make it look like you chose Adonijah. After you promised so many times that Solomon . . ."

"I don't think they'd go that far," he said uncertainly.

Now she was almost shrieking at him. "Don't think they would go that far? Well, they've done it. Let me tell you what's going on this very evening. While we're wasting time talking, that boy Adonijah is having a big feast downtown — all your loyal officers are down there swilling his wine — and proclaiming he is the new king. That's how far they've gone."

"I didn't sign anything," King David said. "Look, I've still got my ring." He held up a bony finger to show her, but the splendid jewel that only the king should wear was gone.

"Uh-oh," he said. "Bathsheba, help me feel around in the bedclothes for it."

◆

"Abishag, Abishag!"

Was it her prince charming come to waken her from an anxious dream into a happy one? "Who's there?"

"Open the door. We've got to hurry."

"What for? Where to?"

"To visit the king."

"I don't think there's much use," she said. But at least, in fact, it wasn't one of those solemn doctors calling on her for another dose of virgin-warmth. When she opened her door a tiny crack, she met the eyes of a very lively boy her own age. Adonijah's favorite brother.

"To visit King Adonijah," he chortled.

"I didn't think he was yet."

"Hip, hip. It's all being settled at his festival tonight. He wants you to come sit beside him at the shindig where it will be announced. Never mind your hair. Looks great as it is. Just slip some shoes on, though."

◆

The slayer of Goliath and hordes of Philistines was afraid of bodily harm if his ring could not be produced. Bathsheba stormed down into sheets and coverlets, pinching and jerking, nudging old shanks this way and that in her frenzy. Those nails of hers might rip the fragile hide from his antique bones.

She lifted his ankles and let them drop in disgust when no flash of gold and precious stone showed what had become of his symbol of authority. Blankets went flying like the skirts of harem dancers as she whipped them one by one through the air and let them fly where they would. From the predatory tension of her curled fingers, he feared that, as a last indignity she would pinch his member off at the root. Instead, she gave his white-haired balls a savage twist.

As she vented her exasperation in this fashion, they heard: the tinkle of the ring as it slid down from its wayward disappearance in the multitudinous coverings and hit the floor. They saw: the better part of the king turning purple and lengthening and curving nobly in the old manner.

"You dawg!" Bathsheba crowed when she recovered the ring and juggled it in the palm of her hand. "You dawg! You didn't really lose the ring at all. You made me think that little bitch had taken it just to upset me. You tricked me into feeling around down there. You old dawg, you!"

In fact, his erection had begun with simple terror. Truly, he had feared she was going to wrench the thing off him and let him go down into the dust unmanned. His prick was a better man than he was. Had translated terror into a promise of resurrection.

Well, who knows how these things happen? In any event, there it stood and, in spite of themselves, man and wife were grinning at its impudence. From his shriveled hams it rose and seemed about to crow aloud.

"Well, what are you going to do about it?" said the king.

"Well . . . I'll send for any concubine you want."

Generosity at such a moment might spoil everything. "Naw," he said. "Only Bathsheba will do."

It was the crisis of her life. Whatever that blind little tower of eager and blood-engorged meat might want, she knew herself old and fat. Fat as a walrus and every pound sagged. Say it with sorrow, the Fair Bathsheba could not deny the ravishment of age. Even in the dimness of the death chamber, it was hopeless.

"All right," she said. "I don't know, David. I just don't know. But I will. Yes."

Within the moment it took the old girl to shuck her clothes a miracle occurred, a miracle so ribald the pinch-gutted editors found no room for it in Scripture.

The death chamber filled with a dawn light. There was a sound of trilling water as from a spring among ferns and wild flowers. A hush and then song. What the eyes of David saw was the body of the original mate, the rib torn from his wounded side. Firm, noble, blushing, roseate, she came to his embrace. It was all shining. Adam and maiden. Hallelujah!

Over the remote dark rim of death, the morning star rose; from the sweet and fearful surf, she came wading to him, the fairest animal to walk on two feet. Smiling, then not smiling. Grave with her single determination to rejoin the flesh from which she had been separated by time and mortality.

In response to such beauty, he could do no less than repeat Adam's holy cry of welcome. Tenderly, he parted her wondrous legs.

Yet, still, before she would let him enter, she held him off for one last question. "Solomon? Will it be Solomon?"

"God's will be done," he said.

◆

It was happening just like in a fairy tale, Abishag would have said. Imagine her, a little nobody really, though men seemed to think she had something going for her — imagine her at a practically coronation party.

Everybody who was anybody in Israel was there. Merchants, soldiers, priests, princes, wives, and concubines to match. You can bet they had all dolled up to greet King Adonijah and his fairy-tale bride-to-be. A terrific turnout. Inside the festive hall as far as the eye could see, there were bobbing ostrich plumes and peacock-feather fans. Abishag might have been the only woman not dressed fit to kill *while* — as any girl would dream it — *while* she was the one who would sit beside Adonijah at the head table up on the platform in front.

Oh, was she glad to be still a virgin! So glad nothing had happened with that shivering old man. It had been a test, she saw now, and she had passed with virgin colors still flying. Now she could be the queen Adonijah deserved and, for the coronation proper, there would be time to get clothes to suit. Something demure but expensive.

Adonijah, bless his heart, seemed tickled to see her so "come as you are" among all the duded-up guests. He had her by the elbow and was introducing her to VIP's she'd never heard of. Adriel the son of Marzillai the son of Barzillai the Heholathite. "Just call me Ad," he said and put a squeeze on her upper arm. Ira the son of Ikkesh the Tekoite. Ahiam the son of Sharar the Hararite. ("Hello, Mr. Wright.") Sizzboomba the son of Scrambleggsy the Hugmetight. Etcetera. Would Adonijah's queen have to get all these names straight?

Abiathar and Zadok were *very high* priests. Abiathar had bad breath and purple bags under his eyes. He looked like he had smelled too much incense in his time.

Joab was a simple name. He looked like one of the farmers from up near home, but mean as a snake. She would remember him in her bad dreams, very likely.

"You're the most ravishing woman here," Adonijah whispered. How's that for a fairy-tale line? Sincere besides, though he had liquor on his breath by the time she arrived.

He could not be blamed for that. Becoming king for a man is like losing virginity for a girl. It only happens once in a lifetime, and both might happen tonight she guessed. She was a little drunk herself with thinking Adonijah, Adonijah, Prince Adonijah, King Adonijah. And his virgin bride. It was certainly worth saving for a big occasion like this.

Now Adonijah was proposing toasts from their table overlooking the packed hall. She sat beside him, thinking her private thoughts while he took care of protocol. He toasted some old priest. A pillar for kings to lean on. He toasted snakey Joab. The sword of righteousness. Defender of the faith, the king's sharp blade. Oh, when would he toast "the loveliest young lady in the room"?

Before he came to that most important toast of all, suddenly, eerily, the crowd grew most awfully quiet. One minute it was the Tower of Babble; the next minute everyone was listening. Now the cheering and singing wasn't in the banquet hall but seemed to be coming from the street outside. All ears were turned to listen to that raucous hullabaloo.

Then everyone seemed to leave their places at the tables on some kind of signal and move toward the front door. "What is it? What's happening?" she asked Adonijah. She honestly supposed it was some kind of climactic surprise he had planned for part of the feast. People love grand surprises, and a new king can afford them.

If he heard her question, he certainly didn't stop to answer it. He stepped on her toes as he scrambled toward the front door with everyone else. She saw him take one glance and then duck back. He started looking for someone in the crowd. Had he swallowed a bone? Was he looking for a doctor? She saw him grab at Joab and shake his husky arm. Joab wasn't a doctor that she had heard of.

She had to pick her own way through the sprawl of guests to find what was happening in the street that had got them so stirred up. Not much of a show out there, really, compared to the tableaux and special acts inside. No acrobats or shimmy dancers or musicians like those who had performed under the smoking torches.

The center of attention seemed to be just a few nondescript people. The prophet Nathan with his head tilted back and his mouth open to pray or give thanks. A few soldiers. Prince Solomon on a mule that looked kind of old and gray. Well, maybe Solomon had come late to pay his respects, which would be nice of him.

He was grinning like a pussycat and holding up his puny arm to show off a ring on his hand. It was a nice ring all right. Very pretty. But what's so important about a ring when many of the guests at Adonijah's party had jewelry as showy as his?

"What's this supposed to mean?" she asked the woman standing next to her.

The woman made a curtsy toward the little group that had caused all the fuss. She said, "It means that Solomon is king. He's wearing King David's ring."

"Oh no," Abishag said haughtily. "Adonijah is king. Everyone knows that. If you'd been inside, you would have heard that much."

"God's will be done," the unknown woman said.

Holding her head up regally, Abishag found her way back into the nearly deserted hall and back to her place at the king's table. Delicately she took small bites of her sherbet. One, two, three, four, five . . . ten . . . twenty . . . As the cup was nearly emptied, her bites were smaller and smaller to make it last until Adonijah came back to sit beside her and go on with the party.

He didn't come, and he didn't come. The torches began to

go out in the middle of the hall and around the remote fringes. There was still music, though the jugglers were packing their gadgets and heading for their transportation, the dancers hurried out with robes pulled up tight around their necks.

But the music went on and on, blue and plaintive and slower as the minutes and hours passed.

Finally, the big black man who led the musicians who had come all the way from Egypt sauntered up to where she sat alone and stood smiling at her.

"You want we should continue the music? Or pack it in?"

"Keep playing," she instructed.

"We can do that. Surely. We can play as long as you want. But, honey, it's getting late. Shouldn't you be going home?"

"Oh, I'm waiting for King Adonijah."

The black man sat down beside her in the chair that had been Adonijah's. In a gentle, fatherly way he put his arm around her rigid shoulders.

"Honey," he said. "Sometimes it's hard to fathom the way things are. They are certainly a bewilderment and a mystery, I will tell you."

"I don't know what you are getting at."

"Honey, the way things are is just too bad."

Bathsheba

———◆———

"SUCH A NICE coronation too," she tells David, sitting in happy fatigue on his deathbed, holding his bony hand to the deep velvet of her bosom. "Everything done in the best of taste."

"A parade?"

"Only a very short one, thanks to God. Oh, I suppose parades are necessary since everyone loves Solomon and deserves a chance to see him. So secluded he has been with his studies."

"Horsemen? Chariots?"

"Such a lovely chariot our Solomon rode out in! Four wheels! A damask canopy with tassels all gold! Our son the king reclining on a white carpet, all dressed in white with a gold band on each arm and such a thin little circlet for a crown so his hair looked very nice. Boys and girls running in front of the horses, scattering flowers. How we all cheered and clapped!"

"The mighty men? Shammah? Zalmon? Eliphelet? Benaiah?"

"I suppose they were there, unless dead by now. Everyone was there. A sea of people. Such happiness! No, I didn't notice particularly warriors. The king intends to de-emphasize the military,

he told me. Then back to the palace gardens. String quartets!
Silk tents everywhere in the shrubbery! Ribbons and streamers!
Exquisite refreshments! Not a bit of drunkenness. Everyone so
polite. So many tributes to the king from the ambassadors. The
Syrian made a lovely speech. Peace will reign in Solomon's era,
he said. What did you say, dearest?"

David's thoughts are in a jumble. He can visualize none of
what she is telling him. Bears and wolves skulk just beyond the
campfire. "Has his work cut out for him."

"Poor old David," Bathsheba says from her fond reverie. "You
never did enjoy it the way you should have. You remember
many's the time I told you, 'Don't you realize you're king? Why
not relax and make the most of it?' Now you have to admit I
told you that, but you were so bull-headed you didn't get all
the good out of your position. And then came the best part.
I think the king must have planned this for a long time but kept
it secret even from me. I'm sure it had been planned since Hiram
was with him four years ago. There were twenty Nubians, all
of them matched for color and height — such a *shiny* black —
they came in carrying what we all thought must be the biggest
cake ever seen. Covered with a cloth to keep it a surprise. Can
you guess what it was? It was a big model of the city Hiram
and his artists had made. It was the New Jerusalem. David, it
was all gold and gardens and pools. Everyone gasped when they
crowded up for a look. So many palaces! Such temples! Orna-
ments on everything! And, David, what made me almost cry,
do you know what he had put? Right next to his own palace?
Almost as handsome as the temple itself? It was a surprise for
me, too, and I cried when I realized what it was. For me! A
palace of my very own! With a walkway above the street, so I
can come every day to see the king! David . . . ?"

The dying old man is snoring.

◆

She has so many marvels to sort out that she sits in the hush of his dying for a long hour until he wakes again. He tries to sit up. The effort is beyond his strength.

"There, there," Bathsheba says. "I'll put this little pillow behind you and you'll be more comfortable. A little broth now? I believe a sip of wine would do you good. I think a little wine to celebrate couldn't hurt. What do you want?"

"Send for him."

"For the king?"

"Get . . . Solly."

"I'll just go see if he's busy. I know he meant to come to you as soon as he could. That was very much on his mind all day. So many well-wishers. Such excitement. I don't think he's forgotten. Not for a minute. He'll be here as soon as ever he can."

"Get . . . Solly."

"Now don't exert yourself too much. Are you sure you're comfortable sitting up? Let me lower you back down again. All right. Just don't get so excited. You thought you were dying yesterday and the day before, too. Why David, you're not dying a bit. I can tell. Soon we'll have you out in the garden again. You can watch the workmen putting in the new flowerbeds. All right, all right. I'll see if he can come now."

She hurries out, and sooner than you would expect, she is back again, following three respectful steps behind her newly anointed son. Solomon has put off his glory. He wears no crown here. His simple blue tunic leaves his plump arms bare, and his face shows nothing but the concern of a devoted son.

"Father?" The tone is almost a plea. If the old man is now at the very threshold of death, it is time for a communication that has never yet passed between them.

"He was awake when I left," Bathsheba says anxiously.

"I'm awake," old David growls. "Things left to settle."

"Yes, Father."

"Adonijah?"

"I have given him a full pardon, Father. He had fled into the temple and taken hold of the horns of the altar. It would be unwise . . . it would be wrong to have slain him there, whatever his crime. He came to me later and promised his loyalty. I told him to go to his house. As long as he is worthy, no harm will come to him."

"Good. Shimei?"

"Yes?"

"He called me a dirty name."

"Oh my goodness," Bathsheba says.

"For which he shall surely die," says King Solomon.

"Good. Joab?"

The new king chews his lip, wondering blankly what he is supposed to say. He cannot speak without a further clue. The dying father has lapsed again into an abyss that may be full of memories or may be as empty as a deep, deep cistern. "Father?"

"Joab."

"Yes. I've been thinking seriously about his rank and his usefulness. Basically I hope to de-emphasize the military and see what can be accomplished by negotiations."

"De-emphasize, my ass. Kill the sonofabitch."

"But . . ."

"He gave me a name for blood-thirstiness. Clean it up. Kill the sonofabitch."

◈

Bathsheba has listened to this exchange with her heart in her mouth. She does not want any ugliness to be part of the wonderful new beginning her son is making.

She keeps such reservations strictly to herself until her husband fades again and she tiptoes out with her son. But in the corridor the impulse to advise is too much to contain.

"He doesn't always know what he is saying anymore," she begins.

"Don't bet on it."

"I think what you did with Adonijah was just right. It was very generous of you, and he's not a bad fellow as long as he knows his place."

"He knows it now. I put my foot on his neck and told him not to wiggle."

"Well. Yes. All right then. But Joab . . . I'll admit I never liked him. I was always afraid of him and what he might do. He's so ugly. Solomon, I'm afraid of him now. He always lands on his feet. He has so many tricks we don't know about. Solomon, leave him alone. He's old too and can't last much longer."

"You heard what Father said."

"At least I wish you'd discuss it with Nathan. He's helped us so often when we had a problem."

"It was Father's dying wish," King Solomon said. "Do you expect me not to honor it?"

Joab

◆

WHAT WORKED for Adonijah might work for me. At least that is my old lady's view. At least, she says, give it a try. What have you got to lose except your head?

Nah. She didn't say the latter. She is a fine woman but not much of a joker. The only fault I ever found in her is she cannot see the humor of a situation.

I had been warned, in so many words and also by my sense of peril, which has often saved me. It is so keen I suppose I should have been born a coward to get full use of it.

This morning, with it all so calm over the city after the coronation and not a breeze ruffling my fig tree, I could feel danger tickling my nape, and there was a smell in the air, kind of like the smell of rust on neglected armor.

With one thing adding to another, I took it also as a bad sign that my recorder Jehoshaphat didn't show up to take down my memoirs. I would like to go back and put in some about Hadad, that King knocked out of that Edomite woman when we were over there on campaign together, way back.

With women in an occupied territory it is always a confusion how feelings will twist in the wind and line up different than you would expect. You have slaughtered their men, right? (In Edom, we had been very thorough, even the boys were scattered on the landscape waiting for us to bury them.) So naturally, the women hate you. Right. They do. But the hate goes through a process in everybody's glands that swells them up and they begin to take over. There was considerable fraternizing, with only a few of our troops having their throats cut for climbing into beds they had made vacant. It is not nice to say, but the smell of death peckered them up. Pity has something to do with it, too.

As truly as I can remember, it was pity got me involved with this bride Buharai, who was also a widow with no one to support her. I got to stopping by her house with raisins and meal for her and her aged mother. They had little choice but to take what was offered and got to be polite about it, and I was welcome in their house. The widow-bride was some looker — tall and well set up with nice tapering legs I got a glimpse of now and then — and I found I had a conflict. I certainly didn't approve of fraternizing. I wanted what I did for them women to be strictly humanitarian.

For once — as never afterward — I mentioned my dilemma to King, who said I saw things exactly right. That it would not be fair to myself, my wife back home, my duty as an officer, to the code of occupation, to let matters go any further. Since he had pretty well echoed me back my own thought in the matter, the next day I rode over to say a sad farewell to Buharai and her mother, taking them a last offering of bread, butter, and honey. The mother met me at the door and accepted the gifts with much gratitude, as usual. On learning I would not be back, she expressed real sorrow that Buharai was not home to add her thanks for all I had done for them. I was sorry too, but relieved on account of my moral conflict.

I was about to ride away when I heard a mule nickering and the animal came trotting up the path from a clump of trees behind their house. Lo, it was King's mule, which had pulled its bridle loose from where he tethered it. Most strange, I thought, but not wanting to leave him afoot in occupied territory I caught the bridle and went down to the trees in search of him.

What I saw first — well, really all I saw — was Buharai's long legs sticking straight up in the air from a green thicket. Her legs in the air, quivering and jerking in a rhythm I could well interpret.

Hardly breathing, I tied the mule up again and went my way. For just the time it took me to gallop a mile, I was fair pissed off. Then with the sweet air in my mouth I laughed and felt grateful. What's a king for if he can't shoulder the conflicts that are too much for his loyal soldiers? It saved me years of remorse, for I had genuinely sympathized with her plight.

What came of King's balling her in my behalf was another of his first-rate sons. A good lad was that Hadad, who subsequently fled down into Egypt, where they have not forgot the good Joseph did them when they needed it. I hear Hadad found favor with the Pharaoh and eventually married his sister-in-law. He has risen pretty high, being down there if we need him when times go bad again. If there was time, I would crowd a lot of such turns of fate in with the main story.

But I got a poor style and Jehoshaphat is absent. I doubt very much that scroll mice have a sixth sense of danger like mine. Probably he had the sniffles or was a little hung over from the wine that went around to celebrate the beginning of Solomon's reign.

I would have also given Jehoshaphat my second thoughts on Absalom. They should be in the record to true up impressions I have given so far. King and Absalom. There is a deep subject, relations between fathers and sons being a matter requiring the uttermost of precision. It is like a blade, you hone it to the best of your ability and yet you take it out another day and you are not satisfied with the edge, until finally the metal has all been ground away and you got only the handle left.

I got, you might say, only the handle left on King and Absalom. I come to the question did I really do what was needful to King when I slew the boy? And there was the other edge of the blade: Did I do what Absalom required?

His string was used up was why I did it. Not with hate, nor with love either. I killed him along with others elsewhere mentioned because it had to be done. But necessary is of the moment you do a thing, while love is not of the moment. It will lapse and come back on you when a thing is done and cannot anymore be undone.

I would like my questions to be on the record, even if there is no answer for them.

◈

My little grandson was put out as well that Jehoshaphat found reason not to come. So it finally dawned on me why the shaver has hung around all these days I have been spinning out my tale. I thought for some of the time it was because he joyed to hear of the famous battles Grandpa had been at with the whistling of spears and the fierce shouting. Or that being dirty-minded, as most healthy boys are in an innocent way, he liked the parts where I would give my surmise about how Bathsheba took her grip on King.

Not that either. The kid was interested in Jehoshaphat's writing. He wants to grow up to be a scroll mouse, too.

So there it is. It makes me sad. What's the profit when you can't be an example to your own blood?

◈

With such gloom in mind I was hardly stirred when Abishai sent word the sentence had been passed on me. What I said and did was more to quiet the old lady than for reasons of survival.

"That Solomon!" she said. "Oh that awful Solomon. But you may have brought it on yourself, saying about him some of the things I heard you tell Jehoshaphat. I should have come out to warn you to be still."

"You should not have been eavesdropping," I said.

She was taking it all too seriously to admit her mistake. "Get word to King," she said. "I don't care if that shrimp Solomon calls himself king now. The other one is still alive for all we know. Call on him and he will see justice is done. You always said he was just."

"I say it now."

"So . . ."

"If women knew what justice is, they wouldn't ask for it."

"For old times' sake then. You have fought together in many battles."

"Yes," I said. "I could remind him he still owes me for that little old girl over in Edom. Yes, I could do some calculating and present him with a bill."

She saw I was making fun, so she said, "Or if he has passed on by now, you can ask Solomon for mercy in his father's name."

"You are right. We just don't know for sure what is transpiring up at the palace."

"Then are you just going to wait here and let them come for you?"

"Not if you have a better idea."

It was her last resource to say I must run to the temple and take hold of the altar. Fear for me was making her crafty. "He would have killed Adonijah otherwise," she said. "Maybe you are right in what you say of Solomon, but he knows it would look poor to slay a man right there at the altar of God."

"Whatever you ask me, I will do it," I promised. "How long am I supposed to hang on to them horns? Will you bring me victuals if it turns out to be a long while I got to stay there where it is safe?"

"Go quick," she said.

Solomon

◆

I SUPPOSE it would be indelicate to start the demolition while pater is still alive to hear it. Thus the masons, carpenters, and gilders languish, and my vision of the city hovers like a motionless bird of prey above the shanties and dusty streets.

And the old fellow lingers on amazingly, hardly breathing at all, but somehow reluctant to let go either his life or the motley architecture of his time. I doubt that he is afraid of dying. Rather, he conceives of death as losing, and whatever else may be said of him, he does not have the habit of losing.

I have finished my speculations on what fills his dying dreams. That intense ego could not be tempted beyond dreams of *The Life of King David.* He is one of those rare mortals whose whole life has been dreamed rather than experienced, intuited rather than planned, capricious with the ineluctable caprice only afforded by the dreams that rise from sleep.

I am a daydreamer by comparison. So be it. I shall have a multitude of compensations that were simply not available to his generation. With Solomon, the time of invention has begun. Every wish will be matched with an appropriate technique. The promise of the Promised Land made visible to every eye. The inadvertency of passion will flower in shows of affordable emotion. The wild asses of the spirit will carry golden burdens for the incorporated state. Art will rule by art, constraining violence by transfiguring it into a continuous dramatic spectacle.

Thus, while my building projects hang fire, I have polished my literary works. I began my collection and refinement of proverbs with the conviction that the ideal monarchy must not depend on the fiat of visible authority or his tax gatherers and men-at-arms. Behavioral conditioning must attune the populace to its new environment.

Of course they bore me, these platitudes, though there is a compensatory low-camp titillation in regarding them as fulfillment of one among my *personae.* Behold Solomon the Square, grave king of Israel, *pater patriae,* taking thought for all strata of his subjects down to the oxen. Codifying rules of conduct for the most banal of lives. Wearing the guise of genial rectitude.

While I . . . !

At least, it must be said of the Proverbs that I have given them an elegant balance. The old vinegar has been handsomely packaged in new bottles. And I shall offer a first collection in the autumn. A limited edition on vellum. Popular editions to follow on state anniversaries. Foolscap versions for use in elementary schools. A little red brochure of *Pensées de* . . . no, *Thoughts of King Solomon.* When they have been fully distributed, the entire police force can be disbanded. Every citizen shall be his own policeman. The savings in administrative cost can be diverted to more alluring projects. Consider how many brass pomegranates can be purchased with the salary of a single constable.

◈

How many discharged constables will pay for the golden masks I shall require for Abishag?

What hallucinatory conceits have spun from the single glimpse I had of her *dos*. What coitus can compare to the *coitus interruptus* of Great Solomon?

Artfully, I have refrained from all opportunities to look the virgin in the face. On my orders, she is being fattened in strict seclusion for the night when we render up our virginities in the ultimate delirium.

There shall be the light of a thousand torches to play over our couch. For I must feast my eyes on every cranny and compound curve of ideal form before I plunge to the awesome contact. Casting my darling into the glowing lava.

But then, even then, the condition of survival is that I must not look on the face of the bride. Hence the masks she must wear in my presence. The perfection of intercourse resides in my conceit that her true face is . . . *Solomon's.* The appearance of a merely pretty girl beneath me would rip the tissue of desire, the sublimating ordeal would be perverted into bestial thrashing, the lineage of the sun would not hive in her virgin womb as my revelation says it must. My great somersault toward divinity would fail and the child be born another mortal.

Therefore a mask of purest gold for Abishag, Abishag, Abishag. Yet I have delayed my order to the craftsman for one reason. I cannot decide if the mask should be plain as the surface of a mirror or modeled with my features. This is too exquisite a consideration to be left to chance — as any artist will understand. I must eke out the decision with care. Meantime

tending to my toil with the Proverbs in lieu of the cold baths
Nathan used to recommend as a bar to self-pollution.

◈

Therefore I was diligently laboring them when B broke in
upon me.

"O King . . ."

"All right, B. What is it this time?"

"I see you're writing. I'll come back another day. Or wait
outside until you've finished."

"Tell me what you need. Just spit it out." I hate to spoil the
old lady's fun, but she can waste too much of my time with these
"O King" and "milord king" flourishes.

"No, I'll wait. I know I mustn't disturb you when the Muse
is here."

"Nobody here but just us royalty, B. What do you want?"

"Go on and finish your verse, at least. I'll just sit over here
by the window and not utter a peep."

"I'd rather you told me now, so we can settle it and you can
go on with your errands."

Oh no. She had plumped herself down at the window by
then and was fiddling with the curtain to let me see she was
determined not to interrupt my writing. I threw down the pen
and took to pacing, though a show of irritation always plays into
her hands. As *mère du roi* she has expanded her repertoire of
annoyances.

"Please," I begged.

"Well, I could just as easily have waited until tomorrow. It's
not that important, really. It's only that I thought I might catch
you before you got tied up with a lot of ambassadors and min-
isters and I don't know what all."

"It happens I'm late already. The king of the Ammonites has
been cooling his heels outside the throne room most of the

morning. So if you won't tell me now what you want, who knows when you'll get a chance?"

That softened her a little. She likes to hear that I'm dealing with other royalty. Makes my being king sound less like fiction, I guess.

"Well, it doesn't seem important at all, but . . ." She took a long cheerful breath as if she had choice gossip to share and said, "It's your brother Adonijah."

"Is he at it again?"

"Not a bit. Not a bit, O King. I think he's secretly relieved that we caught him in time. Before the worst happened. I told him when he came to see me that being king was very hard work. That it required someone who was very wise or it might just fly back in his face. He agreed. No, he's learned his lesson and doesn't want to be king at all."

"What . . ."

"What?"

". . . does . . ."

"Does he want? Well, you'll laugh I'm sure, but I think it's a neat way for things to settle themselves. Somehow, he's taken it into his mind that he can't be happy unless he can marry that little tramp."

"*Which* little tramp?" I demanded — though the sudden on-set of migraine had already told me.

"You know, I thought we were rid of her. After that ridiculous farce with your father. I thought she'd gone back to the village where she came from. No! It seems that someone has ar-ranged for her to hang around Jerusalem, after all. Promised her a career in show business. It might have been poor Adonijah, though he doesn't seem to have much gumption left since you had your talk with him. Probably some disgusting old lecher who . . ."

"Do you mean Abishag?" Even pronouncing her name aloud

seemed to profane the lustrous designs in which she figured.

"Is that what she calls herself? No one ever told *me*. People just spoke of her as 'that virgin.' Well, Abishag then. Rather silly name I think, isn't it?"

I walked back to my escritoire and, to camouflage my trembling, picked up the scroll I had been working on.

"I'd say let him marry her and good riddance to both of them," B advised.

I read my Proverb aloud: *"He that is slow to anger is better than the mighty; and he that ruleth his spirit than he that taketh a city."*

"Why that's very nicely written, Solly. Well put. I think it's one of your very best. I'll remember that one, yes. 'He that ruleth a city than slow to anger.' We could all profit from that principle, I'm sure."

"But," I said, "having been slow to anger, I am now very, very angry."

"I hope not at me, O King."

"What does Adonijah expect anyhow? I spared his life and that is not enough for him. Most people think that life is the most precious of all gifts. But no! He wants 'that virgin,' too."

B was sure by now that I had taken offense at her as well. She said, "I never called her a virgin and I wouldn't believe it if science said so. I think it would serve Adonijah right to have to marry her and live with her in some small town."

"He's not going to live anywhere," I said. "I'll see to that."

◈

Having spoken like a king, I saw to it.

But even with that despoiler dead, I am afraid Abishag is useless to me. The sacred dimension has gone out of reach. The idea of the mask on a plump virgin still appeals, however. I suppose it ought to have my features. Rather stylized so no one but me will note the likeness.

Joab

◆

IT WAS FIRST-RATE thinking for my old lady to figure Solomon the Soft would not send troopers to kill me here in the temple at the altar. Take a woman who never in her life set foot inside the palace and had only crumbs of hearsay about how the anointed arrange things, she did awfully well with what she had to go by. I give her credit as well for knowing my case was not exactly parallel to Adonijah's when he came here. She would not have supposed it would necessarily work out parallel just because the rules are the same. She is smarter than that.

She was smart, but wrong the troopers would not come inside to kill a man hanging to the horns of the altar. For here they are.

I hear the clink of armor and rattle of spears down below the steps in the vestibule and the sound of sandals of a disciplined formation. The priests are chirping like birds that they can't carry their arms in here, and the sergeant is saying that, well, they are going to.

So it is a good thing I came with a knife hidden in my sleeve, which the priests never noted nor tried to stop me. It is a good old knife, and at the poorest, I should be able to take two, three, maybe four of them with me. That is a fine satisfaction to know, and all I could ask for. With luck, I can . . .

No. I am still as tricky as can be, and one man alone has got a certain few advantages when he finds himself amid an armed formation. Whichever way he strikes, he will hit an adversary, while they have to be careful they don't stick each other. With only a broken spearshaft, I have made my way out of a pack of goyim all with swinging swords and left a trail of brains and sundry tissue on my way. But no.

These are good lads doing their duty. I will let the knife fall out of my sleeve.

I said my old lady was smart, and why she talked me into coming here was she knew I had run out my string and wanted me to die in a holy place, and if there is any shame to it, it will be on Solomon, not me. It is like my own thought. Maybe she overheard me say it to one person or another: When you've had your supper, it is time to go to bed.

Should I fight my way out of this one, it would only be to go live somewhere foreign and surely fall into their wicked ways without the support of what is dear to me. That good old fig tree and my grindstone have kept me from many things that would not become a man.

It is much like when I watched that boy Absalom ride off into the forest when he had lost his battle. I knew — *if he did not* — there was nowhere for him to emerge out on the far side of the woods. So I went in after him, the man who sees clear being the one on whom decision always rests.

Yet, like folks say, you come to know things in the Temple which is pure mystery before you arrive there. I know now I did wrong to take Absalom's life, though there was no help for it.

That is why King sentenced me. Not for Abner or Amasa, where I did King's will, even if he was unclear about it himself. As far as it matters, I did the same with Absalom. King could not have continued King with Absalom living on past his rebellion. And without he was King, all his wrongs would have made no sense. Would have added too heavy against him.

But it would have also been wrong for him to forgive me ever for the blood of his son hanging there so helpless in the tree.

In the world as I know it, right and wrong come out to much the same thing. I do not change my saying on that. I only say that beyond right and wrong there is something else we lack a name for and can only admit it is there.

With them coming up the stairs and crowding in formation behind me, I let go my grip on the horns of this altar. They will find no sweat where my palms held to it.

"General," the sergeant says. He starts to salute. Figures now is not the time for such.

"Sergeant," I say.

I see him give the sign and the spears come level.

Solomon

◆

WE SAW MY father the king gather himself for a last worthy effort of his dreaming will — which was feeble enough, to be sure, when it was translated through his vanquished body. Hardly more than a twitch of his neck muscles and the stretching of gray lips, forming a smile if you chose to interpret it so.

We heard him say then, in a surprisingly clear voice, "Don't be afraid, little son. I am come to bring you a light."

Then he died.

Nathan was delighted. He clasped his hands and beamed at me. "What a *nice* blessing, O King Solomon!"

"He was not talking to me," I said.

As I am building the New Jerusalem, I shall have to put up a suitable place to keep Nathan. After all these years, somewhere besides on my back.